Raider watched the whole thing through the telescope. The sheriff parked the wagon in front of the tents. A Chinese man, the head of the family, came out to meet Bridge. They argued when the sheriff flashed some papers at him. The Chinese man waved a knife. Bridge drew on him and shot him in the chest.

Shorty hurried as he rolled back the wagon cover. Raider saw the Gatling gun that had been mounted on the wagon bed. The rest of the family came out of the tents to see their fallen patriarch. Shorty turned the handle of the Gatling. The revolving battery cut the family to ribbons in an instant. The echo seemed to last forever...

J.D. HARDIN

THE BUFFALO SOLDIER

BERKLEY BOOKS, NEW YORK

THE BUFFALO SOLDIER

A Berkley Book/published by arrangement with
the author

PRINTING HISTORY
Berkley edition/February 1985

ISBN: 0-425-07790-X

A BERKLEY BOOK ® TM 757,375
Berkley Books are published by The Berkley Publishing Group,
200 Madison Avenue, New York, N.Y. 10016.
The name "BERKLEY" are the stylized "B" with design are trademarks
belonging to Berkley Publishing Corporation.

PRINTED IN THE UNITED STATES OF AMERICA

CHAPTER ONE

"I don't give a damn if Allan Pinkerton himself is waiting, Doc. I ain't goin' nowhere till Miss Tina here finishes scrubbing my back."

Doc Weatherbee averted his eyes from the spectacle of his partner, Raider, and the naked girl who stood over the tub, rubbing Raider's broad, soapy back. It had taken Doc two hours to find the bathhouse of the Dodge City brothel. Doc exploded a sulphur match and torched the end of his Old Virginia cheroot.

"You'd better hear me out, Raider," Doc said, slipping the silver matchbox into the pocket of his silk vest.

"Stop blowin' smoke in here," Raider barked. "That stuff would gag a Kiowa buffalo skinner. And shut that damned door before I catch the grippe."

Doc slipped into the bathhouse, closing the door behind him. Raider's girl stood up and smiled at the well-dressed gentleman. She was oriental, Doc thought, probably Chinese. Chubby-faced, plump, smooth-skinned, brown nipples, shoulder-length shiny black hair. It seemed odd that Raider, who topped six-feet by several inches, should end up with such a tiny woman. But then, Raider showed a predilection for anything female. Doc removed his pearl-gray derby and bowed to the bare lady.

"Doc Weatherbee," he said. "So pleased to meet you."

"Don't start that dandy stuff," Raider growled. "The next thing you know, ole Tina here'll be talkin' like the queen."

"Weatherbee want bath?" Tina asked.

Doc blushed. He almost dropped the cigar from his lips.

"That won't be necessary," Doc replied.

"Try it, Doc," Raider said, grinning. "They got a few chippies here that'll turn over the spit and back."

1

"Raider, we should discuss the business at hand."

"Business!" Tina squealed. "I get pretty girl for the pretty man. Business! Yes!"

"Raider!"

"No, honey. Doc and me work together. We just ran down these two coyotes who thought stealing was better than honest labor. You understand, Tina?"

"Yes. Pretty girl."

She started for the door. Doc stepped into her path, blocking her exit. Her cherubic form was dangerously close. He detected the scent of her hair, rare and inviting like the far-off breezes of Polynesia. Her washcloth was dripping on Doc's five-button Melton overgaiters.

"Raider..."

"Don't get his shoes wet, Tina," Raider said. "I'll never hear the end of it if you ruin those spats. Get over here and do what I'm paying you to do."

Tina resumed her position, wetting the cloth in the steaming tub and running it up Raider's sore back. In pursuit of two highwaymen, Raider had flown off the back of a moving buckboard, landing with a thud in a ponderosa pine tree. When the washcloth hit the gash on his shoulder, Raider flinched.

"Damn it, girl, take it easy."

"I brought a tincture for you," Doc said, slipping a bottle of red liquid from his neatly tailored suit coat.

"You ain't puttin' that crap on me!"

Doc tossed the bottle to the naked courtesan, who uncorked it and dumped the tincture onto Raider's wound before he could stop her. It burned like hell. Raider's howling brought a slight smile to Doc's lips.

"To promote healing," Doc said wryly.

"Tina, bring me my gun."

"Raider, Allan Pinkerton is coming to St. Louis. He wants us to be there by tomorrow morning."

"We can't ride all that way by tomorrow."

"The train," Doc replied.

"I hate the train, Doc. The smoke makes me—"

Tina poured a bucket of steaming water over Raider's black hair. Raider shook his head and sat up. He turned to look at

Doc, as if what Doc had said finally registered in the thick, durable skull that seemed to be made of iron.

"Pinkerton himself?" Raider asked. "The boss man?"

"Yes," Doc replied, reading Raider's black eyes. "It does seem odd that he would come out into the field, as it were."

"Must be something important."

"Or personal," Doc said. "After all, he is a man of honor."

"Aw hell."

"Raider, don't get testy."

"Doc, can't you just go and see him alone? I mean, you could send me a wire and I can meet you. Ain't I earned a few more days here with Tina?"

"I'm sure you have," Doc replied. "However, if you enjoy your work, you'll comply with Pinkerton's mandate."

"Aw, you know how I get around the boss. He always scowls at me, like I was a Injun or something. And I always open my yap and say the wrong thing."

"Just cease from utilizing your jaw muscles and you'll be fine," Doc insisted. "Now, if you'll vacate that tub, we'll be on our way."

"Er, Doc, did you bring your wagon?"

"Yes, why?"

"So your mule is out front?"

"Of course," Doc replied.

"Maybe she could use some company for a while," Raider said.

"What are you driving at, Raider?"

"Well, me and Tina here got some business to do."

"Business, yes!" the girl said.

"But, Raider . . ."

"Ain't right to start something without finishing it," Raider said. "Don't worry, we'll be on time. Vamoose!"

"Did you ever see a man so big?" Tina said, reaching into the tub and fondling the floating appendage between Raider's legs.

"You have ten minutes," Doc grumbled.

"And shut the door behind you!"

Tina slipped over the edge of the wooden tub. Her dark, fuzzy wedge was steaming from the hot water. Her eyes were bulging with anticipation as she guided him into position.

"You gonna be all right, girl?"

"Soon I will see," she replied.

She splashed in the water, smiling as she thought of what she would tell the other girls.

Raider had always hated riding on trains. His legs were too long to be comfortable, and the air always smelled like smoke-stack sulphur, which was worse than the smoke from Doc's cheroot. The seats weren't much softer than a saddle, and the ride was just as bumpy. Doc didn't seem to mind trains, but then Doc wouldn't mind anything that put a burr under Raider's saddle.

Of course, as Doc had pointed out many times, you could sleep on a train car, something that was difficult on the back of a horse. But Raider always found that when he finally managed to drift off, it was a fitful, rocking slumber that left him frazzled and nauseous the next day. The worse thing was falling asleep in a contorted position, only to have Doc nudge him six hours later at their destination. Raider didn't feel right being taken somewhere in his sleep. It seemed like a cheating way to travel.

"I hope to goodness that we don't draw train duty," Raider growled as they stepped on the platform in St. Louis.

"Don't complain," Doc replied. "The railroad is happy to give us free passage. They're always glad to have a Pinkerton aboard."

Raider snorted like a wild animal.

"And I'd certainly pity the ne'er-do-well who disturbed you in your precious sleep," Doc said. "You can be wrathful when you've just woken up."

"Dang gone it, what's that smell?" Raider barked.

"Only the city," Doc replied.

They started along the platform.

"Where we supposed to meet the boss?" Raider asked.

"At a private dwelling," Doc replied. "I have the address."

"This ain't a ambush, is it?"

"Hardly," Doc replied. "One of Pinkerton's old chums from Chicago is now the deputy police chief of St. Louis."

"Let's move out," Raider said. "Might as well get this over with pronto."

"Not just yet," Doc insisted. "We still have a couple of hours before the meeting."

They were both dusty from the train ride.

"What are we gonna do until then?" Raider asked.

"I suggest we find a hotel and spruce up a bit before we—"

"I ain't wearin' no starched collar, Doc!"

"Raider, if you can't throw off this surly disposition, I shall be inclined to use unmitigated force."

"What?"

"Shut up before I shoot you!"

A household servant ushered Doc and Raider into the neatly organized study of the deputy police chief. The heart redwood walls of the den had been decorated with framed citations and honors. A huge oaken desk filled up most of the bright room. Doc smiled. Of course Allan Pinkerton would have a huge oak desk to sit behind—the symbol of his unquestioned authority. Three chairs rested in front of the desk, two for Doc and Raider and the extra one for a third party. Raider tugged at his starched collar and flopped in a chair.

"Is he late?" Raider asked.

"Not yet," Doc replied, glancing at the clock on the wall behind the desk. "Leave that collar alone!"

Raider wouldn't wear a suit coat, but Doc had talked him into shining his boots and buying a new pair of trousers and a leather vest. With the addition of a starched shirt, fresh from the laundry, and a string tie, Raider looked almost human, Doc thought. It was also the first time in several years that Raider was not wearing the .44-caliber pistol strapped to his side.

"He's gonna be late," Raider said.

"It's three minutes to eleven," Doc replied. "The appointment isn't until eleven."

"A double eagle says he doesn't make it before the clock strikes the hour," Raider said.

"I'll mark that," Doc replied.

"He has to walk in before the clock finishes . . ."

Raider smiled as the large hand drew closer to the twelve, moving imperceptibly on the white clock face. As a bell began to sound the hour from the clock's inner workings, Raider smiled and extended his open palm. On the ninth chime, Allan Pinkerton's towering frame filled the doorway of the den. They stood up immediately, as if a judge had just entered the room.

"Weatherbee," said Pinkerton. "I see you arrived as scheduled. Well done."

Pinkerton strode past them and stood behind the desk. A second figure moved into the room, sliding behind Doc and Raider toward the empty chair. A husky black man in a neatly pressed suit stood next to them.

"Gentlemen, meet Alexander Othello Thomas," Pinkerton said.

Doc offered his hand to Thomas, marking the details of his appearance. His grip was firm, the hand weathered. Salt and pepper in his hair, betraying his age—Doc guessed forty-six. Broad, lined countenance. A fine suit with mother-of-pearl buttons, probably purchased in Louisiana, near New Orleans, where that fashion abounded.

Thomas looked him directly in the eye and spoke in a clear, resonant voice. "Pleased to meet you, Mr. Weatherbee," he said.

"Doc."

"Yes, of course," he replied. "And you must be Mr. Raider."

Raider's black eyes went back and forth between Pinkerton and Thomas. As he shook hands with the black man, his stomach churned so loudly that Doc could hear the commotion. Pinkerton turned a scornful gaze on the big man from Arkansas.

"Is there something wrong, Raider?" Pinkerton asked.

Raider shook his head.

"Does Mr. Thomas make you feel uncomfortable, Raider?"

"No," Raider muttered.

"I beg your pardon," Pinkerton insisted. "I didn't hear you."

"No, sir. He doesn't make me uncomfortable."

You do, Raider thought.

"Raider is just getting over a fever," Doc offered. "He's not quite himself."

"Let's be thankful for that," Pinkerton said. "Be seated,

gentlemen. We have business at hand."

Raider tried not to slouch when he sat down, but his long legs extended in front of him, causing him to feel awkward in the small chair. He turned his Stetson around on his fingers, trying not to look at his superior. Doc thought it strange that Raider feared their employer. They had faced much worse terrors than Pinkerton.

"Have you filed the case journal from your last assignment?" Pinkerton asked Doc.

"Yes," Doc replied. "It was posted the day before I received your wire directing us here. Had I known we would be meeting, I would have delivered it to you personally."

"You simply followed procedure, Weatherbee," Pinkerton replied. "Can't be too efficient for me. Rules are rules."

The big man leaned back in the chair behind the desk. Thomas was watching Pinkerton with a complacent expression on his face. The look of a man who had found the answer to a problem, Doc thought. Raider was looking at his own re-flection in the sheen of his boots.

"I wouldn't have come to St. Louis ordinarily," Pinkerton started. "But Mr. Thomas here is a friend of mine."

Raider glanced up.

"It's no secret that I held to abolitionist views before the war," Pinkerton continued. "My home was used as a stopping point on the Underground Railroad during the civil conflict. More than one fugitive slave stayed with me back then. Mr. Thomas here was among those men."

Pinkerton stood up—for effect, Doc thought. He touched a balled fist to his chin. Raider sat up straight.

"I sent Mr. Thomas south after he came to me," Pinkerton said. "But when he left Illinois, he went as a member of the Union army. At the end of the war, he remained in the infantry to serve in the western army. He has distinguished himself in battle against the Confederacy and against the Apache tribes. He is a good man. His word is to be trusted implicitly."

Pinkerton was staring at Raider when he made the last statement.

"Would you like to proceed from there, Mr. Thomas?"

"Yes, thank you," the black man replied in a gentle tone.

He had benefited from some formal education, Doc thought. He pondered before he spoke, and then he articulated in a concise manner. He sounded like a country lawyer to Raider.

"As Mr. Pinkerton remarked, I have served in the army of the United States since 1862. I was twenty-nine years old when I first put on a blue uniform," Thomas said.

Doc did the mathematics in his head. Thomas was forty-six, a lucky but educated guess earlier.

"Originally, I am from Louisiana..."

Right about the buttons, too.

"...but I escaped from my former...master...to fight for the Union and for freedom. I owe everything to Mr. Pinkerton here. He urged me to enlist in the infantry. Of course, even then we were kept in our own regiment."

"We?" Doc asked.

Doc saw the peculiar flashing in Thomas's eyes. Raider had seen the same expression in the face of an Apache Indian named Growling Bear. Raider was pretty sure it had been hatred then.

"Men of color are restricted to separate companies," Thomas said dryly. "Even when we were fighting in the Indian wars, the Negro men weren't allowed to associate with the white soldiers."

Thomas ran a hand over his short-cropped hair. He paused, looking away for a moment, composing himself in the wake of an onrushing memory. Pride returned to his expression.

"It didn't matter to us, however," he continued. "Even when we were left to bring up the rear for the white regiments, we did not complain."

"Why'd they make you ride drag?" Raider asked.

"You don't know?" Thomas said bitterly. "Colored soldiers aren't as brave as white infantry. No, we usually came in behind them to pick up anything left behind. Mainly we looked for anything that had been pilfered from the army or from settlers. It was our responsibility to give any booty to the commander. Only once did I distinguish myself on the battlefield, and that was quite by accident."

"Perhaps you should explain the situation at hand," Pinkerton said. "My train will be leaving shortly, and I'd like to make sure that there are no misunderstandings before I depart."

Why did Pinkerton keep looking at Raider? Doc wondered.

"Yes, I will get to the point. A year ago, I retired from the infantry. I had saved some money over the years, and I was as homesick as a man could be. My brother had sent me an occasional letter, but those were vague and stopped altogether after a while. When I returned home to Louisiana, I discovered why he had not written to me."

He took a deep breath.

"You can't imagine what I returned to," Thomas said. "My family, what was left of it, had been reduced to hungry share-croppers, at the mercy of a new kind of overseer. And if a black man tried to reach beyond his station, he met with the disapproval of men in ceremonious white robes."

"Lynchings?" Doc asked.

"And worse," Thomas replied. "But no matter. I was determined to leave the South. I realized that I missed the western territories. And it didn't take a lot of persuasion to convince my kin to follow me. My brother came, with his wife and her sister. We bought a wagon and started west with my savings to sustain us.

"When we reached Dodge City I discovered an opportunity to purchase a tract of land. I met with a representative of the Hutchison Western Title Company, a Mr. Wilson Samuels. He claimed to have a hundred acres for sale in northern New Mexico, fifty miles south of Colorado."

"Near Raton?" Raider asked.

"Yes, that's the nearest settlement, I believe. We were happy to have our own land finally. Our journey was filled with anticipation. My brother had been worried because we purchased land so far north. But he was not disappointed. Our land was covered with thick grasses—blue grama, galleta, and buffalo. The soil was rich and free of stones. We planned to farm and raise cattle. The growing season was shorter in the northern part of the territory, but my brother was sure he could make the adjustment."

"Quite a change from Louisiana," Doc said.

"Yes, until the sheriff arrived from Raton to evict us from our own land," Thomas replied.

"What the hell?" Raider blurted out.

"Yes, my thoughts at the time," Thomas said.

"Why did they turn you off your land?" Doc asked.

"No explanation, except that the sheriff claimed we were homesteading illegally. He gave us two hours to clear out."

"Weren't you issued a deed to the property by the title company?" Doc asked.

"No, only a bill of sale," Thomas replied. "Samuels promised to deliver the deed within two months. He claimed that legal papers take time to clear through the territorial governor's office. I was wrong not to insist on a deed before I gave him the balance of the money. But he assured me that the bill of sale was enough."

"Have you sought a judgment through the proper authorities?" Doc asked.

The angry gleam surfaced again in his eyes.

"The U.S. marshal advised me to forget about my loss and just clear out," Thomas said. "It seems that men of color are not privy to the protection of the law—east or west."

"May I look at the bill of sale?" Doc asked.

Thomas removed a folded document from his coat pocket. Doc examined it closely. It recorded the sale of a land tract to Alexander Othello Thomas by the Hutchinson Western Title Company. Mr. Wilson Samuels was the representative of the company. No purchase price was indicated.

"The sheriff tore off the section stating the monetary particulars," Thomas said.

"And you just took it?" Raider asked.

"I preferred not to ruffle the local authorities," Thomas replied. "I have seen what can happen to a Negro man when the seeks justice. Instead, I sought he help of an old friend."

He talks like Doc, Raider thought.

"Do you have something to say, Raider?" Pinkerton shot back.

"It's just a damned shame that Mr. Thomas here was bamboozled by this Samuels," Raider replied.

"No sympathy necessary," Thomas rejoined. "I feel comfortable in bringing the problem to Mr. Pinkerton. He assured me that he would assign his two best men to the investigation."

"He said that?" Raider asked.

Pinkerton's face turned an indignant shade of red.

"Don't get excited, Raider," he growled. "I merely said that I would assign the best *available* agents."

Raider slumped in the chair, trying to hide the residual grin.

"Gentlemen," Pinkerton said. "You are to assist Mr. Thomas in establishing enough evidence that will enable him to regain his land or money through proper legal recourse. Act as you would in any standard investigation. Keep me posted. And"—directed at Raider—"follow the letter of the law and standard company procedures."

"Of course," Doc said.

Again to Raider, Pinkerton remarked, "Understood?"

Raider bristled. "I got something to say here."

Doc could not stop him.

"I got a feelin' in my craw that y'all are holdin' some kind of grudge against me. What are y'all worried about anyway?"

"May I?" Thomas asked.

"Of course," Pinkerton replied.

"Mr. Raider," said Thomas, "the accent of your voice makes it clear that you are from the southern half of the Mason-Dixon line. I've encountered many men from the South who cannot tolerate the presence of a Negro man. More than once your kind has called me a ni—"

"Now hold on right there, Thomas," Raider said.

"Raider," Doc interjected, "perhaps you should—"

"No, Doc, they're gonna hear me out. Now, if Mr. Pinkerton says for me to take a case, I don't care two hoots in hell who the client is or where he comes from. I'm gonna do my damnedest, 'cause I always do. I ain't called nobody no names. And if you don't want my *kind*, Mr. Thomas, you say so now. 'Cause in the field, we got to cover each other."

For a moment, everyone was silent.

"I'm sorry to have judged you," Thomas said finally. "No offense."

He extended his hand.

"None taken," Raider replied, gripping it.

Doc sighed. "Well, we're all agreed then."

"Fine by me," Raider rejoined.

Pinkerton, who was unusually calm, took an envelope from his pocket and tossed it to Doc.

"Your back pay and expenses," Pinkerton said. "I want you to be ready to get under way within the hour. Mr. Thomas will wait here until you are prepared."

"We won't be long," Doc replied.

"Gentlemen," said Allan Pinkerton, "I want this matter taken care of as soon as possible."

"Assuredly," Doc said. "Assuredly."

As soon as they were outside, Raider loosened his collar and tossed the string tie in the street.

"I'm glad that's over," he said.

"You certainly spoke your piece back there," Doc said.

"Why'd they come at me like that?"

"They wanted to see how you felt about helping Thomas," Doc replied.

"Was I out of line?"

"No, I think Pinkerton respected you for speaking up, and it certainly gave Thomas an insight into your character."

They started for the hotel.

"How do you really feel about accepting a Negro client?" Doc asked.

Raider shrugged. "Hell, Doc, you and me been up and down both sides of creation. We seen nearabouts every kind of man and woman to be knowed. Ole Thomas there ain't no varmint."

"No, he's undoubtedly educated," Doc replied. "An interesting man."

"Even if he does talk like you."

Doc laughed.

"And I'd say he got the short end of it," Raider said.

"Yes," Doc replied. "Just like you."

"Me?"

"Yes, where's my twenty-dollar gold piece?" Doc asked.

"What the hell are you talkin' about?"

"Pinkerton was right on time," Doc replied.

"Shit!"

"Settle up, Raider."

"Just take it out of my back pay," Raider replied.

"All right, but we'd better hurry. We'll have to catch the next train back to Dodge City. I believe our first stop will be at Hutchison Western Title Company."

"Damned train," Raider said, scowling.

His stomach was already churning.

CHAPTER TWO

"What's he doin' in here?" asked the train conductor.

He was pointing toward Alexander Othello Thomas, who sat with Doc and Raider in a private compartment, paid for by Allan Pinkerton himself.

"Coloreds are supposed to ride in the colored car," the conductor said. "It's railroad policy."

"How'd you like to lose that finger, mister?" Raider growled from underneath his Stetson.

"I beg your pardon."

Raider stood up and looked down at the rather weak-chinned conductor.

"This here gentleman is with us," Raider said. "Doc, show him our credentials."

Doc politely withdrew the documents that stated their status and purpose, flashing them at the conductor.

"Pinkertons, eh?" the conductor said. "He a prisoner?"

Again he pointed at Thomas.

"I thought we'd settled that finger down," Raider scowled.

The conductor put his hand in his pocket.

"Mr. Thomas is our associate," Doc said.

"Yeah, any problems with that?" Raider rejoined.

"No," the conductor replied. "But he still can't eat in the dining car with you."

"Look here, gopher-face," Raider started.

"Excuse me, Raider," Thomas said. "I'll speak for myself. I don't mind forgoing the dining car."

"Yes," Doc agreed. "It would be better if you brought us our meals in the compartment."

"Yeah," Raider said. "Seeing's how our bosses are good

14

buddies, we'd hate to tell him that we didn't get . . . what was that, Doc?"

"First-class service," Doc replied.

"What'll it be?" Raider asked.

"I'll see to it," the conductor replied, stiffening with professional pride.

Raider ushered him out of the compartment and sat down. Thomas was smiling. Doc looked out the window at the receding daylight.

"The Great Missouri Plain," Doc said. "Tell me, what is the terrain like in New Mexico?"

"Well, we're in the northern section," Thomas started.

"Oh no," Raider groaned. "I can see you two are gonna start jawing it up about ever'thing. I'm gonna see if I can find me a pretty lady to sit next to."

He reached for the compartment door.

"Wait," Thomas said. "There's something I must tell you."

Raider leaned back. Thomas was not smiling now. He was staring away for a moment. Mustering strength for a confession, Doc thought. And so early in their journey for complications to set in.

"I have to make you aware of something in my past," Thomas said. "It may surface later. I don't want any surprises. I don't like surprises."

"Neither do we," Raider replied.

"As I told you in Mr. Pinkerton's office, I was in the infantry of the western army," Thomas said. "We were a service platoon. We followed the white regiments, calvary and infantry alike, usually in charge of the mess. When I retired as a corporal—"

"Corporal?" Raider said. "And you was in for fifteen years?"

"Sixteen," Thomas replied.

"How come you never made sarge?" Raider asked.

"How come the conductor gave me a hard time?" Thomas said. "My color, Mr. Raider. Simply that. I cooked the white soldier's food, and they went out into battle. I ate their garbage and was glad to get it because I had known a rougher time."

Doc shifted in his seat, contemplating what it must be like to be owned by another human being, to be someone else's property. There was no frame of reference, unless his servitude to Allan Pinkerton counted. But even at that, he could leave the service anytime he chose. Pinkerton didn't really own Doc and Raider. He only acted that way.

"If you detect a note of bitterness, gentlemen, then you can consider yourselves perceptive," Thomas continued. "One does not eat the dust of the world without getting a dry mouth. You long for things. Nothing ambitious. Not wealth or fame. You long for the warmth of the fire with a kettle of beans hanging over the flames, the smell of your woman, your children. Things I will never have because my woman was taken to the house of the overseer to work in the kitchen. I went to war shortly after that."

He took a long pause, during which Raider examined his face. Too thoughtful, Raider decided. The kind of man that tried to figure things out. That could drive you stark raving mad, trying to figure things too much. You could think something to death.

"As I told you before," Thomas continued, "our Squad often picked up the debris after a skirmish. We found everything from Indian trinkets to fine China pilfered from settlers. In Shoshone villages we saw a whole way of life being stamped out. And we only shook our heads and rummaged through the waste. You got used to it. Shifting dead bodies like they were sacks of flour. We usually got burial detail too. You get hard after a while, that's the only reason I was able to do what I did."

"And what was that?" Raider asked too impatiently.

"They were chasing Red Wolf then," Thomas said.

"The Apache?"

"The same," Thomas replied. "He had gone against the tribe by stirring up the few angry braves who wanted to follow him. A treaty was imminent by then, but Red Wolf didn't want peace. They mustered a patrol at Fort Belknap to stop Red Wolf and his renegades. At the time, several details were on patrol, so they were short of men. My commander suggested that I come along. He thought me capable. If he had only known how capable I really was."

"So what happened to Red Wolf?" Raider asked.

"We caught him at Three Wells," Thomas replied. "He wasn't trying to hide his tracks. He wanted a showdown. He got it. We backed him into a ravine and cut him up good with our Henry rifles. Forty-four-caliber slugs. I fired too. Who were the savages?"

"In all due respect," Doc said, "I hardly think killing Red Wolf qualifies as a misdeed. Barbaric perhaps, but it was your duty."

Thomas shook his head.

"You don't understand," he replied. "Something else came later. After Red Wolf was killed, we offered the other braves a chance to come back with us. As they were rounded up, I was commanded to search the area for booty and plunder. Red Wolf had been up and down the territory, so it was assumed that he had a large cache of supplies. It turned out to be much more. In a wall of the ravine, deeper in the rock, was a narrow recess, a cave just big enough to hold a small man or a woman. Red Wolf had carelessly hung a blanket over the entrance. It was late afternoon when I found it, but I could still see what shined in the shadows."

He leaned back and smiled ironically.

"The Spanish searched the West looking for the Lost City of Gold," Thomas said. "But I found it. Red Wolf must have robbed a church. Gold candlestick holders, a rosary of solid gold, a chalice. Quite a lot, in fact. Over a thousand dollars when I finally melted it down and sold it."

"Sold it!" Raider bellowed.

"I never reported that cache of gold," Thomas said. "It's the only truly dishonest thing I've ever done in my life. I tore the blanket away and covered the entrance with rocks. When I came back to the regiment, I said that I had found nothing."

"And you got away with it?" Raider asked.

"I did," Thomas said softly. "I retired two months later and went back to that little hole in the wall. I took my gold and cashed it in. I didn't tell Mr. Pinkerton because he is a man of high principle and he might not appreciate my predicament. But I'm telling you because, as I said, I do not like surprises."

They were quiet. Doc was stroking his chin, gazing out the window. Raider was looking at his boots. Both were asking themselves what they would have done in Thomas's situation. Doc started the dialogue that rendered their judgment.

"Raider," Doc said. "Mr. Thomas has confided in us a secret that might incriminate him. He obviously trusts us and respects us enough to be truthful. What do you think?"

"Hell," Raider replied. "Now let me get this straight. Thomas, you found the gold in that ravine, right?"

"Yes," Thomas replied.

"Nobody else but you? Hmm, then I guess that makes it your gold, don't it? I mean, you didn't rightly know who it was stolen from. Did you?"

"Can't say as I did," Thomas replied.

"Well, now," Raider rejoined. "Seems to me—and you can shush me, Doc, if I'm wrong—seems to me that men find gold all the time. Only then it's called prospectin'. You think Thomas here was prospectin' when he found that gold?"

"I suppose you could interpret it that way," Doc replied.

"Then I'd say you just hit the mother lode, Thomas," Raider said. "So keep your yap shut before ever'body finds out about it."

"Yes," Doc replied. "Consider it your business. I doubt if Red Wolf stole the gold himself, since the artifacts were religious."

"Why do you think that?" Thomas asked.

"Well, was there a church or mission anywhere within a hundred miles of Red Wolf's territory?" Doc offered.

"No," Thomas replied.

"Maybe Red Wolf got it from a traveling priest," Raider said.

"Possibly," Doc replied. "But more likely Red Wolf simply discovered a cache of gold relics and icons that were taken from an early church of the territory. Spanish missions were quite common two hundred years ago. Three Wells, where you found the gold, was the sight of such a mission. Now, given that the Indians rose up against these early missionaries, one can assume that Red Wolf's cache of gold was placed in that cave by a priest who might have been hiding the sacred gold from an attack by Indians."

"Makes sense," Raider said.

"You simply found a vein that had been undiscovered for nearly two centuries," Doc replied. "You were ordered to find and return Red Wolf's plunder. Since he had not originally plundered the gold, then you did not disobey your commander at all."

"Thank you, gentlemen," Thomas said. "Thank you."

Raider peered into his tired eyes. Tears were falling onto his angular cheekbones. Thomas was crying, tears of joy right there in front of them.

"Aw hell," Raider scowled. "I got to stretch my legs and see if I can get into trouble."

Trouble was a poker game in the adjoining private car. As he stood between the cars with air rushing all around him, Raider detected the sound of chips clinking together as they hit the felt surface of a gaming table. When the train slowed, the sweet music stung his cowboy's ears like a siren's call. As a man who cared little about money, Raider was not afraid to make a wager. And his pockets were full of back pay. He had a lucky feeling in his gut. After the bet he had lost to Doc, his luck had to swing back the other way.

Raider steadied himself as the train rumbled through the plain. He was trying to decide how to make an entrance. Night wasn't far off, and he sure as hell didn't feel like listening to Doc and Thomas. Those two would be jawing all night. Again he heard the faint click of chips. Or were those gold pieces?

"I gotta try it," he said out loud.

The handle on the compartment door was not locked. Raider turned it and stuck his head cautiously through the opening. Some men might not take kindly to an intruder. He half expected to be shot at. But no one blasted him. Instead, the four card players only looked up at him. Raider smiled to show them he was not the enemy.

"Sorry," Raider said. "Guess I was headin' the wrong way up the creek."

"Come in if you're comin'," said a short, pudgy man with a curled mustache. "Close that damn door, too, either way."

Raider slid into the compartment and secured the door. Someone at the table had some money, Raider thought. The compartment was fancy, like one of those houses where Doc visited one of his young widows. The fat little man turned his attention back to his cards. He didn't seem annoyed or daunted by Raider's abrupt entrance.

"Playin' draw?" Raider asked.

No one answered. The fat man held his five cards close to his chest, his mustache twitching back and forth like a cat's tail. Judging by the pile of discards, the draw had come and now the four players were making their final bets. A stack of double eagles rested in the center of the table. Another pile clinked under the fat man's fingers. He plucked off forty dollars—two gold pieces—and tossed it into the pot.

"Call your twenty and bump you twenty," the fat man said.

"Too rich for me," said a dapper, thin-faced dude.

"By me," rejoined a gray bear of a man.

"You ain't scarin' me," said a kid whose smooth face was hidden under the brim of a floppy felt hat. "Your forty and forty more."

The little man smiled.

"Call," he replied, answering with two more gold pieces.

"Two pair," the kid said. "Aces over queens."

He made a premature gesture for the pot. Raider counted a hundred dollars on the table. The fat man stopped the kid.

"Hold your taters, boy," the man said. "Aces up is a might powerful, but it don't beat three deuces."

The kid seemed stunned for a moment, but he took it well finally. He laughed and leaned back in his chair. Raider still couldn't see his face under the hat. One dim lantern hung over the table, putting the losers in shadows as the winner pulled in the pot.

"Drag, lucky, drag," the kid said good-naturedly.

"Hell, nobody draws three ducks," the slim man rejoined.

"Glad I got out of that one," said the gray bear.

The fat man little man looked up at Raider.

"Name's Barnwell," the man said. "That's what you can call me. You mighta heered of me. Made a dolluh or two up in Abilene. Been shipping my cows north, south, east, and west on the railroad. People says I'm smart, but hell, I still feel like a cowpuncher. What they call you, boy?"

"Raider."

"Well, that's Slim, cause he's so skinny, and this is Jeremiah, my foreman. Kid's name is Johnny. We playin' a honest game."

"I can sure see that," Raider replied.

"What line you in, mister?" Slim asked.

"Guess I'm a Pinkerton," Raider replied, gauging their reaction, which was again undaunted.

"I'm sure as hell glad we runnin' a honest game," Barnwell laughed. "And you welcome to join, boy. We could use some new blood."

"Yeah, sit next to me," the kid said.

"Don't mind if I do," Raider replied.

His heart was pounding as he slid into the chair. He transferred the money from his hip to his shirt pocket, leaving a few dollars to bet on the table. Again he looked around the table. They seemed honest enough. He'd try a few hands and see how it went. Barnwell handed him the deck.

"The new man rolls 'em," Barnwell said. "Your deal, boy."

"Stud poker, five cards," Raider replied. "That all right?"

"Name the game and the stakes," Barnwell said. "We friendly and honest."

"Five-dollar ante," Raider said. "Five-dollar bet. Ten on a pair. Twenty on the last card. No limit on raises. Any objections to that?"

"Fine by me," the kid said.

The other two men nodded.

"Hell, I like this boy," Barnwell chortled. "I might just put him to work for me."

"How's that?" Raider asked as he shuffled.

"Yeah, maybe he ain't no cowpuncher," the kid rejoined.

"Not punchin' cows," Barnwell replied. "When we git to the end of the line, I'm buyin' part of this railroad. And if I lose, at this table, I'm gonna put ole Raider here to work for me and then fire him."

They all laughed as Raider dealt out the unlettered cards. In front of every player, he put one up and one down. The slim fellow drew a deuce up, the bear a four, and Barnwell got a queen. The kid was counting the diamonds on a ten.

Raider rolled an ace for his up card. Another ace was buried beneath it. Swing back, Lady Lucky, he thought.

"The bullet bets," Barnwell said.

"It's worth five," Raider replied.

"I'll see it," the kid said.

"I'm in," from Slim.

"Me too," from the bear.

"Raise five," Barnwell said. " 'Cause I don't believe ole Raider has another ace down there."

"Pay and see," the kid replied.

Raider tried not to smile as they all stayed with him. He didn't raise back until he drew the third ace on the fourth card. Only Barnwell stayed with him, playing a pair of queens over fives. Raider dragged two hundred dollars when he revealed the buried ace after the last card.

"Nice hand," the kid said.

"Beginner's luck," Barnwell chortled.

All the same, Raider thought, a fellow with a due streak of luck could walk away from a train game with a sizable winning. Just load up and then play cautious until things got tiresome. And when he wanted to leave a winner, just say, "Gentlemen, this is my stop," and get up from the table.

"Draw poker," the kid said, tossing out five cards to each player. "No limit, ante five, open for the pot."

Raider was staring again at two of the aces he had just played.

"Open for twenty," he said, trying not to smile.

"Doggone it," Barnwell snorted. "Somethin' tells me it's gonna be a long evenin'."

Doc and Thomas rested quietly for a while, dozing and looking out of the train window as the plain began to grow darker. Morning would break before they arrived in Dodge City. Doc continually glanced at his client, wondering if he might solicit more information from the well-mannered black man. As Thomas had been so willing to tell them about his found fortune, Doc decided to continue in the spirit of inquiry.

"Mr. Thomas," he said finally. "My partner is easily given over to trusting his instincts. I, however, would like to appease my curiosity by asking you a few more pertinent questions. That is, if you don't mind."

"I'd be willing to answer any questions you might have," Thomas replied.

Doc politely offered Thomas a cigar, and both men smoked as Doc directed his first question.

"Please do not be offended," Doc started, "but you seem to have benefited from a formal education. Your diction and manners are certainly beyond that of—"

"A Negro?"

"I was going to say an army corporal," Doc replied. "Did you attend school at all?"

"Not formally," Thomas replied.

"But how did you cultivate such a refined manner?"

"I suppose I have to thank my former masters," Thomas replied.

"I beg your pardon?"

"I was owned by two men," Thomas said. "You see, when I was on the plantation, I worked in the fields. When my woman was taken to the kitchen, and forced to sleep in the house, I tried desperately to see her. I was young then and much more bullheaded. When I persisted, my first master put me on the auction block. I was strong and fetched a handsome price. But I was not taken as a field worker the second time. Instead, a young New Orleans lawyer took me as his butler. He had lost his wife in childbirth with their second daughter, so he needed someone to oversee the household. I was put in charge of the other two servants."

"Interesting," Doc said. "How did you fare in your new position?"

"Not well at first," Thomas replied. "But my new employer was a good man, and he had patience with me. He forced me to sit in on his daughter's school lessons. I resisted at first, but I quickly saw the benefits of being able to read and write, especially when you are dark-skinned in a white country."

"Yes, I can understand that."

"I doubt it," Thomas replied flatly.

"And you escaped from your second—"

"He urged me to go," Thomas replied. "I left with a sense

of regret. Of course, he had to report my escape, but he waited a week to do it. All white men aren't evil."

"Thank you," Doc replied. "Tell me, you are a smart and resourceful man—why did you stay in the army?"

Thomas laughed. "Reading Plato and Homer hardly substitutes for a trade, Mr. Weatherbee. The army was something of a home, I suppose. I got used to it."

"And rich," Doc replied.

"Touché."

They were respectfully silent for a moment.

"If I may?" Doc said finally.

"Surely."

"You made a comment in St. Louis that has stuck in my mind. You remarked that your Negro company only distinguished themselves once in battle. Would you care to elaborate?"

Thomas sighed and leaned back. He loosened his collar and placed his ribbon tie on the seat next to him. After rubbing his face with his hands, he began to speak without looking at Doc.

"We were in the Southwest," Thomas said. "Somewhere between Arizona and New Mexico. The Apache were at their worst then. We were looking for Cochise, had been for a month. When we didn't find him, General Kearney ordered us to make camp below an Apache village near Lordsburg. Word was sent out that if Cochise did not surrender by the next afternoon, then the village would be destroyed. Since most of the men were following Cochise, the village was mostly women and children."

"Grisly business," Doc said. "What happened?"

"Cochise didn't surrender," Thomas replied. "So that afternoon the white regiment made good on the general's promise. They came back right before dusk. My platoon had supper waiting for them. We were ordered to go back up to the plateau and search the remains of the village.

"As we ascended the rise, I saw dust to the west of us. A war party of Apaches came riding out of the setting sun. They were orange in the twilight. I'll never forget that. I sent a rider to the regiment below and then turned to face the attack."

"Good God, how many were there in your platoon?"

"Twenty at best," Thomas replied. "Twenty against a hundred braves. We simply fell to the ground at the edge of the rise and stood them off until the regiment was mustered from below. I sustained several wounds, and all but three of us were killed."

"You must have received a medal for your bravery," Doc offered.

"No," Thomas replied. "In fact, officially I was reprimanded for shooting without direct orders. Privately, the general thanked me, but that was my only recognition."

"Hardly fair, I'd say," Doc rejoined.

"Hardly," Thomas replied. "But you get used to it when your skin is another color."

Doc did not feel like asking any more questions. Talking to Thomas was unsettling. Too much injustice to deal with. *"All men are created . . ."* He thought about it.

"A fine cigar," Thomas said finally. "Virginia tobacco?"

"The best," Doc replied.

Doc pulled his gold watch from the pocket of his silk vest. Eight-thirty. Suddenly he thought of Raider, who had been gone for more than two hours. The flash of uncertainty in Doc's countenance was detected by Thomas.

"Something wrong?" he asked.

"No," Doc replied. "Only a bit concerned about my partner. He should have been back by now."

"Shall we look for him?"

"No," Doc said. "I'll leave him to take care of himself. He's usually more than capable."

Usually. And then there were times when things got a little out of hand. But Doc didn't like to think about those times. It only made him feel uneasy.

CHAPTER THREE

Raider had played his luck just right. As the good cards kept coming, the columns of twenty-dollar gold pieces had swelled to an impressive height. All in all, he figured to be about five hundred dollars ahead. At one time he had been up almost seven hundred, but he had to trickle some of it back into the game, playing smart but staying with the others so they couldn't accuse him of sandbagging. Even at that, he had almost a thousand dollars with his back pay, some in script paper, but most of it double eagles supplied by Barnwell.

Barnwell didn't like to play with anything but gold. Raider watched him, looking for the sudden wild eyes of a loser. But Barnwell was a cowboy who had made good, one of the West's gamblers who had won big. He only kept after Raider in that good-natured ribbing way, laughing all the time, drinking from a bottle of red-eye.

"Hell, Raider, if I'd knowed you was gonna be so lucky, I wouldna asked you to sit down with us," Barnwell chortled. "You whuppin' me somethin' terrible."

"Lay off," the kid snapped without warning.

Barnwell's foreman stiffened, and the slim man's eyes turned nervously toward the kid. Raider slid back from the table, his hand automatically reaching for his side. But his .44 wasn't there. He had left it in the compartment with Doc. A dumb oversight.

"You been ridin' him all night," the kid said to Barnwell. "Pinkerton here done stayed in every hand. So why you on him, old man?"

"Better watch your mouth, son," Barnwell replied, no longer smiling.

"I might just shut yours, old man!"

26

"Simmer down," Raider said, grabbing the kid's wrist. "We're here to play cards, boy. Five stud, no limit. Is that okay?"

The kid nodded and Raider let go. While the kid huffed, Barnwell laughed it off. As Raider rolled the cards, he kept an eye on the kid. The kid had been betting heavy, and his luck had been up and down. Still, he had a pretty good pile of money in front of him, since he had taken five of the last six hands.

Barnwell had lost heavier. He had been throwing a double eagles like they were wooden nickels. Barnwell should have been riled, but he only continued to smile. Raider rolled the up cards and glanced at the kid, who showed an ace.

"Your bet, kid," Raider said. "Ace looking at us. What'll it be?"

The kid kept looking at the cuckoo clock on the wall of the compartment. Raider felt feverish all of a sudden. Something didn't feel right. He pushed his chair back a little more and challenged the kid to bet.

"What'll it be, boy?" Raider asked.

"Don't call me boy," came the sharp reply.

The kid came up out of the chair. His face caught the light of the lantern. Flash of cold steel eyes under a smooth, sweaty forehead. His hand was full of a Navy Colt .36 percussion loader. Raider measured the distance with his eyes, wondering if could jump the kid and avoid taking a slug.

"What the hell's wrong with you?" Barnwell asked. "You plumb loco or somethin'?"

The cuckoo clock sounded the midnight hour.

"Time for you to raise your palms, biscuit eaters," the kid drawled. "You too, Pinkerton. This here's my game. Navy Colt beats four aces. Changes my luck, too."

"You're makin' a bad mistake," Raider said. "You ain't lost much, if you lost at all. So lower that steel barrel and we'll forget about this whole thing."

"Just shut up, Pinkerton," the kid replied. "This ain't between you and me. But if you give me any trouble, you'll be the first one I drop."

The kid backed up and looked out the window. Raider

shifted his body weight forward, but the kid swung around and stopped him with a look. They were glaring at each other as the five-car train slid to a steaming halt.

"Looks like my boys showed up on time," the kid said. "You, Pinkerton, pick up those saddlebags under my chair. And if you do anything but throw them on the table, you'll be pickin' lead out of your face."

Raider went down slowly and picked up the saddlebags with his right hand. He thought about flipping the saddlebags into the kid's face and then following with a lunge. But it was too risky. Raider had enough scars on his body. He wasn't ready to take on the Colt. He put the saddlebags in the middle of the table.

"Good," the kid said. "Put everything from the table on the left side. All of it."

The slim man and the foreman didn't have much to steal. Raider was the big loser. As he scooped his winnings into the saddlebag pouch, he wanted to tear the kid's head off. It would have been a different story if Raider had remembered to wear his gun. It was the last time he would ever be caught without it, he vowed to himself.

"I think you done riled our friend here," Barnwell said.

The kid slid around behind Raider, keeping the bore of the Colt trained on his head.

"Now it's your turn, old man," the kid said. "Take the bag from the Pinkerton and fill it with everything you got."

For the first time, Barnwell's jester face turned serious.

"You're loco," Barnwell said. "You better just take what you got here and clear out."

A pistol shot from outside startled them. More gunfire followed. The kid put the pistol bore to Barnwell's temple.

"I know you got a strongbox, old man," the kid said. "You're takin' it to Dodge City to pay for your share in this railroad. I want the strongbox—now!"

More shots from outside, the loud chortle of a rifle. Someone screamed and shouted the kid's name: *Johnny*. The kid looked toward the window. Raider decided to move then. But so did Barnwell's foreman, who dropped his arm quickly, popping a derringer from his sleeve into his palm. But the kid was quick too.

The Colt erupted in a loud clap that deafened Raider for an instant. Blood oozed from a hole in the foreman's chest. Raider reached for the derringer, which had fallen on the table. He felt the pearl handle until his arm went numb. A burning slid up his shoulder where the kid had hit him with the butt of the Colt. Raider tried to turn, letting off one shot from the derringer. The Colt barked again, and the burning was suddenly on his scalp. Raider fired the second shot from the derringer as he went down. Then he was on the floor, unconscious of the confusion that surrounded him.

Raider knew the trouble was over the moment he opened his eyes. The shooting had stopped, but the air still smelled of black powder. Raider listened for a moment, hearing muffled voices from outside. He tried to sit up, but the sharp pain from his scalp slowed him down. Someone had wrapped a white bandage around his head. After assessing the pain, he decided that he had felt worse in his life. Finally he sat up.

"Just about thought you was a goner," said Barnwell, who sat opposite Raider. "Me an ole Slim put you on the bed there. Your partner doctored you. Said the slug just grazed you. Said you had a damned hard head too."

"Doc," Raider groaned. "Where is he?"

"Still out yonder, I reckon," Barnwell replied. "He just up and took charge of everythin' after he run off them varmints. He some kind a dandy, ain't he?"

"Got any whiskey?" Raider asked.

Barnwell tossed him a bottle of red-eye. The amber-colored liquid burned Raider's throat and guts. Two more gulps drove away most of the pain in his skull.

"Your buddy said you's lucky to be alive," Barnwell said. "I guess my foreman warn't so lucky. Dead as a door nail. I loved that ole boy. Knowed him most of my life. Now he's layin' up there in the mail car. Don't seem right, somehow."

Raider threw his legs over the side of the bed and tried to stand up. After a weak-kneed attempt to walk, he grabbed the wall and tried to catch his balance. He took another drink from the bottle, drew a few deep breaths, and then somehow managed to get out of the compartment and off the train. He walked toward the sound of Doc's voice. Doc was helping an old woman into the next car. Thomas was standing behind him, wielding a lever-action rifle. Raider staggered toward them, holding his head.

"I see you've returned to the land of the living," Doc said when he saw his wounded partner. "I suppose you don't remember anything."

"Don't act like it's my fault," Raider replied. "I didn't ask them boys to rob the train. Besides, I remember every damn thing. Some green kid bushwhacked us and ran off with our poker money. He took some strongbox from Barnwell too."

"Correction," Doc replied. "He only got the poker money. And he was riding with a gang."

"How did Barnwell save the strongbox?" Raider asked.

"Well," Doc replied, "when Thomas and I realized the train was stopping, we loaded our weapons and discouraged the thieves."

"How many were there?" Raider asked.

"Five, counting the man who shot you," Doc replied. "Did you recognize the man in the poker game?"

"No."

"You were winning, weren't you?" Doc accused.

"What's that supposed to mean?" Raider muttered.

"You aren't at your best when you're at the gaming table," Doc replied. "I've warned you about gambling."

Raider looked at the rifle on Thomas's shoulder and tried to change the subject.

"You get that rifle in the army?" Raider asked.

"Yes," Thomas replied. "Why?"

"Good gun," Raider said. "Haven't seen a Henry rifle in a while. Y'all shoot any of them thieves?"

"I believe I hit one of them," Thomas said. "Although he managed to stay in the saddle."

Raider licked his lips and looked out into the dark plateau where the train had been stopped. Even though the night sky was covered with stars, there still wasn't much light on the plain. Raider turned and bolted up the steps into the car.

"Where are you going?" Doc asked.

"I gotta get my gun," Raider said.

"What do you intend to do?"

Raider came back out of the car, strapping on his holster.

"I'm gonna have me a look around," Raider replied. "Thomas, see if old Barnwell will give you that lantern that was hanging over the poker table."

"Yassuh," Thomas replied sarcastically.

"Aw hell, man, you know I didn't mean it like that," Raider said.

"Of course not," Thomas replied. "I'll get the lantern."

"You won't find anything," Doc said. "It's too dark."

"Maybe, maybe not," Raider replied. "But if Thomas there winged one of them, they mighta dropped my money. See if you can delay the engineer for a little while."

Thomas came back with the lantern, and Raider stumbled down the incline of the track bed. Doc and Thomas watched as the lantern moved slowly through the darkness, swinging back and forth over the ground. Doc spoke to the engineer, who agreed to the delay. He then rejoined Thomas, who had kept an eye on Raider.

"What's he looking for?" Thomas asked.

"I'm not sure," Doc replied.

"Look, he's stopping. Now he's swinging the lantern. He wants us to join him."

"I was afraid he might find something," Doc said. "Shall we?"

They walked slowly toward the dim lamp, feeling each foot of earth with one cautious step after another. Raider was motionless, standing over something large. As they came into the circle of the light, they saw the body lying on the ground. Thomas had sent a bullet through the man's neck, rupturing the jugular vein.

"You shot true," Raider said. "He didn't last long."

"God forgive me," Thomas replied.

Doc knelt over the body, trying to examine it. The light was not good enough. He took the lantern from Raider, but that didn't help. He needed more light and a better space for a thorough and professional investigation.

"We'd better drag him back to the train," Doc said finally.

"You two go on," Raider replied. "I'll take the lantern and look around some more."

"What do you have in mind?" Doc asked.

"This boy was ridin' a horse," Raider replied. "If I can find it, I can pick up the trail at daybreak. Maybe before, if I find some good tracks. I can get my money back and meet you back in Dodge City."

"Out of the question," Doc replied.

"They got my money!" Raider barked.

"That is inconsequential," Doc replied. "Your loss is totally unrelated to the case at hand. We have no resources to aid in pursing the men who robbed this train."

"What are we s'posed to do?" Raider cried. "Just take it?"

"We'll file a report with the marshal in Dodge City and with the office in Chicago. If the railroad wishes to hire two other Pinkerton operatives, I'm sure Mr. Pinkerton can assign worthy men. As for us, we have to stay with Mr. Thomas here."

"Doc, I'm out a thousand dollars! Those buzzards picked me clean. I'm busted."

"You brought it on yourself by gambling," Doc replied. "I've no sympathy for blatant stupidity."

Raider wanted to gripe, but he realized that Doc was right. Raider had taken his chances with Lady Luck, and he had lost. She had dangled the bait in front of him by letting him win, and then in the next roll of the dice she had kicked his ass. All of his back pay was gone. He felt like a green, mule-headed cowpuncher.

"Take his arms, Doc," Raider said. "I'll get the feet."

"Perhaps our dead adversary will render the identity of the man in the poker game," Doc replied, taking his end of the bulky cadaver.

Back in Barnwell's compartment, they spread the body on the floor. The grizzled dead man wore stiff, dirty clothes under his stained duster. Doc slowly went through his pockets, coming up with a knife, two derringers, and a bundle of papers. Raider's money was not on the body.

"Who is this son of a bitch?" Barnwell asked.

"We shall see," Doc replied.

Doc unfolded the bundle of papers. He held up a wanted poster that bore a general likeness to the dead man. WANTED, DEAD OR OTHER. RIO JOHNSON, FOR KILLING AND CRIMES RELATED. $100, AMERICAN. Doc showed the poster to Raider.

"Do you know him?" Doc asked.

"Rio Johnson, huh," Raider replied. "Only thing I ever heard about him was that he was ridin' with Johnny Denton."

"That kid!" Barnwell cried. "His name was Johnny. Told me Johnny Yakel was his name."

"The Oklahoma Kid," Raider said.

"What was that?" Doc asked.

"Johnny Denton," Raider replied. "Calls himself the Oklahoma Kid. Used to operate around the Oklahoma border. I reckon he's done come a little farther west."

Doc turned to Barnwell.

"How did this Johnny get into your poker game?" Doc asked.

"Hell," Barnwell replied. "Ain't no secret I got a private game. He just showed up, like Raider here. We was short a hand, so I let him come on. He had plenty of money."

"I'm not surprised," Thomas said suddenly.

"What you talkin' about, boy?" Barnwell asked.

Ignoring Barnwell's slur, Thomas raised a faded newspaper into the light.

"It seems this man's gang robbed a bank in Missouri several weeks back," Thomas said. "Our friend here saved the evidence in print. It's all right there. I wonder if he could even read."

"Interesting," Doc rejoined. "And Johnny Denton used part of the money to buy himself into your game, Mr. Barnwell. Tell me, was there any way for Denton to have known about your strongbox?"

"Hell, I got a big mouth, Mr. Doc," Barnwell replied. "I guess ever'body knowed I was up to somethin'. I just sold a passel of cows in St. Louis. Word gets around."

"Well, if you'd like to hire an agent to pursue an investigation, simply wire the Pinkerton office in Chicago," Doc said.

"Ain't no need to do that," Barnwell replied. "I got my money. Ain't nobody gonna bring back my friend."

"We're going to file a report with our office and with the marshal in Dodge City," Doc replied. "In the meantime, I suggest we move this corpse into the mail car with the other one."

"They can keep each other company," Barnwell said in a halfhearted attempt at humor.

"Wait a minute," Raider said. "I want to do something about my doggone money."

"Forget about it, Raider," Doc replied.

"Aw hell."

"I'm willin' to offer a reward for saving my money," Barnwell rejoined.

"We aren't allowed to accept gratuities," Doc replied.

"Not so fast, Doc," Raider cried.

"Help me with this unfortunate soul," Doc ordered.

"Aw hell!"

"The money's gone, Raider," Doc insisted. "You'll only torture yourself thinking about it."

As Raider hoisted the torso from the floor, he gnashed his teeth together, thinking about what he'd like to do to that Oklahoma Kid. Raider didn't care what Doc said. Sooner or later he was going to come face to face with Johnny Denton and his thousand dollars. And when that happened, Raider planned to be holding all the aces.

The Oklahoma Kid had delayed the Dodge City train by two hours. The stationmaster at Dodge City was not too surprised or worried that the train had not arrived at six A.M. as scheduled. Two hours late was almost on time. Sometimes the train was two days behind schedule, and since Dodge City was the last stop, the stationmaster didn't sell tickets west. On days when there wasn't a train, the stationmaster served as the postal officer. He was an important man in the community.

Dodge City was changing, the stationmaster thought as he walked toward the station. The railroad was changing it. All the west was different with the train. And men like the stationmaster had come west to administer that change. A man could still be important if he had the right job. A man in the right position, an important man, could still make a fortune for himself, the stationmaster thought as he unlocked his office.

Two cowboys were sleeping on their saddles under the ticket window. The stationmaster took his time opening shop and eventually sold them two tickets east. Couldn't go west yet from Dodge City. The tracks were going down, though, winding westward toward Santa Fe. Be able to go clear across to California one day. Probably only take two weeks to do it. But the cowboys didn't listen, they just paid for their tickets and went back to sleeping on their saddles.

After the stationmaster opened the postal office, he brushed his black vest and straightened his visor cap. He was the only railroad representative in Dodge city, but he was going to look official. He also found a certain excitement in the people who came through the station. They were often interesting and usually dangerous.

And there was always news from the train when it arrived. Like the story of how the Pinkertons and the Negro drove off the Oklahoma Kid and his gang, which the conductor related to the stationmaster as he handed him the mailbag after the train finally pulled in. Was the Okalahoma Kid heading to Dodge? they wondered. Hadn't he been seen around before? Didn't the marshal run him off? The news made the morning brighter. The stationmaster was primed for Doc and Raider's entrance. He was more than happy to assist two Pinkertons.

"Can I help you gentlemen?" he asked the well-dressed man in the pearl-gray derby.

"I take it you are familiar with the local authorities," Doc replied.

"Yes, sir."

"There are two corpses in the mail car of the train," Doc said. "They need to be examined by a coroner, if you have one, and buried in any case. I shall file a full report with the marshal."

"I'll go myself," the stationmaster replied. "Doc Riley signs all the death notices."

"Before you go, please put this with the mail," Doc said.

He deposited an envelope on the counter. Doc had been unable to sleep on the train, so he had written a report of the attempted robbery for Allan Pinkerton. The report said Raider had assisted in driving away the assailants, with no mention of the poker game or Raider's unfortunate head wound. Doc had been kind as well as efficient.

The stationmaster picked up the envelope and put it on a postal scale. "That'll be ten cents," he said. "It's a little heavy."

"Give the man a dime, Raider," Doc replied.

"Me? Hell, that's all I've got."

Raider pulled two nickels from his pocket. Doc took them from his hand and put them on the postal counter. The stationmaster smiled and dropped the coins in his strongbox.

"They say y'all had a time of it," the stationmaster said.

"Some," Raider replied.

"Is it true a nigger really shot Rio Johnson?"

"Hey, boy..."

"Raider, let it go," Doc said. "A black man did assist us. And I would appreciate it if you would help me with two things."

"Sure," the stationmaster replied. "What can I do for you?"

"I'd like to know the location of the marshal's office."

"Down the street, across from the hotel."

"Thank you," Doc said. "And tell me, have you ever heard of the Hutchison Western Title Company?"

"Can't say as I have," he replied. "Haven't seen any mail for an outfit named that. Keep my eyes open though."

"Thank you, you've been most helpful," Doc said.

Doc turned and went outside, where Thomas was waiting. Doc was moving fast, as he always did when he got onto a case. How could he be so fresh after not sleeping? Raider's body was aching for a hot bath and a warm bed with a soft woman in it.

"Slack your heels, Doc," Raider said. "My head is pounding."

Doc and Thomas were halfway up the wooden sidewalk that led the length of the main avenue.

"You should get a powder from an apothecary," Doc said.

"I need some sleep," Raider replied.

"I wouldn't mind sleeping myself," Thomas said.

Raider came up beside Doc, matching his brisk stride.

"Can't our investigation wait?" Raider asked.

"I would like to clear up a few things first," Doc replied.

"Where are you going?" Raider asked.

"To find the Hutchison Western Title Company," Doc said. "And I have to see the marshal, too."

"Do we have to come with you?" Raider asked.

"No, not really," Doc replied. "In fact, it might be better if you didn't. I may not confront them right away with Mr. Thomas's bill of sale. We may want to catch them off guard. I suggest you take Mr. Thomas and find a place to sleep."

"Where?"

"Where you always go," Doc replied. "One of your bordellos should serve nicely."

"With Thomas?"

"Surely they can't be that picky about a man's color in the places you frequent," Doc replied. "No offense meant, sir."

"None taken," Thomas rejoined.

"Hell, Doc," Raider said in a low voice. "I ain't got no more money on me. Could you see fit to—"

"Naturally," Doc replied.

Doc reached into his coat pocket and pulled out his thick wallet. He gave Raider fifty dollars in script. Raider didn't know it, but Doc always held out fifty dollars from Raider's pay. Raider never counted his money, so he never missed it. Inevitably, Raider would squander his earnings and have to touch Doc for a loan. Doc learned early on in their partnership that Raider seldom paid back his debts, so Doc simply took payment when he handled their salaries. He also began the policy of withholding and loaning Raider his own money.

"Don't spend it all at once," Doc replied. "Now, I suggest you return to that establishment where I found you bathing with the Chinese girl. It looked clean, and it will be easier for me to find you if I know where you are."

"All right, Doc," Raider replied. "Anything else you want me to take care of?"

"See to Judith," Doc called as he started off down the sidewalk. "And stay out of trouble if you can."

"Are you sure you don't want Thomas to come with you?" Raider shouted.

But Doc ignored him.

"Who's Judith?" Thomas asked. "A lady friend?"

"Judith is about the most stubborn dad-burn mule on the face of God's green earth," Raider replied. "The only thing stubborner is Doc himself."

Thomas clapped Raider on the shoulder with a friendly hand.

"I do believe you're stuck with me, Raider," Thomas said.

Raider grunted. "Can you ride a horse, Thomas?"

"Expertly," Thomas replied.

"Come on, then, let's get over to the livery," Raider replied. "We're gonna need horses."

"And we have to attend to Judith, of course," Thomas rejoined.

Raider laughed. "Hell, I might just shoot that fly-dipped critter and dress it out for jerky meat."

Thomas wondered if Raider was kidding. Raider started toward the livery, which was on the other side of the street. Thomas followed after him with his rifle still on his shoulder.

"Listen, Thomas," Raider said without looking at him. "On that holdup at the train. You done good helpin' Doc."

"Wasn't it you who said we had to cover each other in the field?" Thomas replied.

"Yeah, I guess. I just wish you'd shot the boy who took my money."

"Well, if we see him, I'll be happy to loan you my rifle," Thomas said wryly. "At any rate, thank you for the words of encouragement."

"Come on," Raider said. "Let's saddle up and ride."

CHAPTER FOUR

Doc Weatherbee was not in love with Dodge City. Despite the local residents' enthusiastic attempts to talk up the town as a center for the union of East and West, Doc loathed the dusty, windswept streets and brown-planked structures. Rough, dirty places like Dodge City made Doc wonder why he had left the great eastern seaboard with its civilized cities—New York, Providence, and his own beloved Boston. Spring rains never turned the byways of Cambridge into impassable strips of mud. As the gray clouds rolled in off the plain, Doc turned up his collar, dreading the precipitation that would follow the cool, humid breeze. Suddenly Doc felt tired and hungry and confused.

A deputy marshal had listened to Doc's story about the holdup of the train. Things had been quiet around town, so the marshal had gone hunting for a couple of days. Doc had written up an official report, and the deputy had witnessed it. He was not surprised to hear that the Oklahoma Kid was involved in some nasty business. The Kid had been around the territory of late, and the deputy had a couple of posters on him. Doc took the poster with the likeness of Johnny Denton so Raider could make a positive identification.

The deputy was also sure that the Kid would not show up in Dodge, not after robbing a train that was heading in the same direction as the law.

"What about the reward on Rio Johnson?" the deputy asked.

"Take it for your trouble," Doc replied.

"We can always use it. I'll see to it that Johnson gets into Boot Hill all right. Anything else I can do for you?"

"Are you familiar with a local enterprise called the Hutchison Western Title Company? Or an agent of that firm named Wilson Samuels?"

"Can't say as I remember coming across either name," the deputy replied after some thought. "You know what this Samuels fellow looks like?"

Doc gave him Thomas's description of Samuels: "A dapper man who takes a great deal of pride in his personal appearance. Thin mustache and face. An affected, almost lisping way of speaking. Heavy scent of talc and shaving lotion about him. Prone to formal dress and manners."

"Seems to me there's been a lot of men like that around lately. Eastern boys lookin' to find the motherlode one way or another. This got anything to do with the Oklahoma Kid?"

"Nothing at all," Doc responded. "I'm working on another case entirely."

"Well, if you need me just holler," the deputy said. "We got respect around here for you Pinkertons. Fact is, I been considerin' signing up myself."

Doc gave him the particulars about the Pinkerton Agency and then left the marshal's office, requesting upon his departure that the deputy look through all town records for any evidence of the Hutchison Western Title Company. Doc wondered if the request would be honored. Sometimes the local constabulatory was less than cooperative, often to the point of conspiracy in the wrongdoing. Doc trusted the U.S. marshal more than a local sheriff—at least the marshal had to answer to the territorial governor's office.

Outside on the wooden sidewalk, Doc reexamined the bill of sale for the land that Thomas had purchased and then lost. The bill was a neatly printed, official-looking document that listed a Dodge City address under the letterhead. Quickly Doc discovered that the address turned out to be the hotel across the street from the marshal's office. He decided to check in. He needed a room for the night anyway.

After signing the register, Doc identified himself to the desk clerk and asked if he could look over the records for the past two months. The clerk replied that he was sure it would be all right, but he would have to check with the manager, who was out of the hotel. Doc understood and politely went up to his room to spruce up.

The accommodations were clean and cramped. Bowl and pitcher for washing and a well-made bed. Doc brushed his coat and hung it on a nail on the door. Then he washed his face and hands, using the stiff towel to dry himself. After combing his sandy hair, he fell back on the feather mattress, exhausted but unable to sleep. His mind didn't feel like slowing down.

The Hutchison Western Title Company was bothering him a lot. Either the locals were covering up something or the company simply did not exist. No mail from the postmaster and no trouble with the marshal's office. Doc needed to ask Thomas several unasked questions. The damned incident on the train had distracted him too much. It was time to balance the scales.

The desk clerk knocked on the door. Doc told him to enter, and he came into the room carrying the guest register. The manager had vowed total cooperation with the investigation. Doc thanked the clerk with a dollar and asked if he could examine the register by himself. The clerk quickly left, as if he was glad to be out of the room.

Doc opened the leather-bound ledger. Thomas had received his bill of sale on the twelfth of the previous month, so Doc looked carefully at each entry from five days before up to the twelfth. He compared the register signatures to the writing of Wilson Samuels. If Samuels had not registered in the same name, Doc might still be able to detect a similarity in the handwriting. Samuels had given the hotel as the address for his dealings, so it was a good chance that he had been there. Doc had neglected to ask Thomas where they had done business.

On the eleventh of the month, a Mr. Stephen Winston had registered his name in the guest book. The first two letters of both names caught Doc's eye. He compared them to the signature of Wilson Samuels. The "S" and "W" were similar in both signatures. S and W. A vain touch by a man who thought too much of himself. It was a trail that only an expert might follow.

Doc ran his fingers over the imprinted title at the head of the bill of sale. Mr. S and W had gone to a lot of trouble to print up an official-looking bill of sale to fool wary buyers. *Printed! Of course!* If the perpetrator had used a local printer, then the printer might have a record of the transaction.

Doc dressed and hurried back down to the desk. As he returned the register, he asked the clerk if he remembered Stephen Wilson. The clerk did not recall the gentleman until Doc gave him Thomas's description. Winston had registered three times in the past six months. The records indicated that he had stayed only until the next day on all three occasions.

"Do you remember if he met with anyone?" Doc asked.

"Maybe," the clerk replied. "I can't be sure though. I don't usually pay attention to our clients' business."

Doc thanked him and headed for the street. Mr. S and W had done business on three previous occasions. Maybe Thomas wasn't his only victim. Doc felt better that something was unfolding. He smiled as the deputy marshal approached him on the sidewalk.

"Couldn't find nothing about no title company," the deputy said.

"No complaints?" Doc asked.

"Not in my office," the deputy replied. "If anythin' turns up I'll let you know. You stayin' at the hotel?"

"Yes," Doc replied. "And if you will, watch for any disgruntled settlers who may be heading back east. I've reason to believe that Wilson Samuels, alias Stephen Winston, may be swindling sodbusters out of their hard-earned money."

"Not round here, he ain't," the deputy huffed.

"Of course not," Doc replied. "He's only using Dodge City as a front. The real damage is done in New Mexico Territory."

"That makes sense," the deputy rejoined. "They tell me New Mexico is as wild as Dodge City used to be."

"Possibly," Doc said. "Tell me, is there a printer hereabouts?"

"End of the street," the deputy replied. "Near the edge of town. You'll see it. Better hurry. Looks like a storm's comin'."

As Doc headed for the printer, he pondered the multitude of questions to ask Thomas. Questions that should have been asked in the beginning. Doc thought about going after Thomas right away, but he decided to tie up a few loose ends first. Thomas and Raider could rest until Doc was ready to find them.

Hard, gray Kansas rain was pelting the ground as Raider and Thomas rode toward the cedar-planked, two-story house just a mile beyond the town line. The more upstanding citizens of Dodge City liked to keep Claire and her girls hidden in the rare stand of cottonwood trees away from the city. Claire ran a nice clean house. Doc was always bitching about Dodge City, but Raider thought of it as one of his favorite stops on the trail.

Raider's bay gelding splashed in the puddles that were already forming on the muddy turf. Thomas, who had purchased a chestnut mare, rode behind Raider, catching clods of murk and mire from the hooves of the gelding. He swung to the side away from the spray. Both men were soaked and dirty by the time they reached Claire's stable.

"Where are you, Little Joe?" Raider called as he swung out of the saddle. "Wake up, Little Joe."

Rows of horse stalls ran the length of the structure on two walls. Claire liked to provide a secure place for her customers' horses. No one had ever lost a mount while he was upstairs in bed. Raider called again into stable. From one of the stalls came a short black man who tended to the animals of Claire's patrons.

"I'm right here, Mr. Raider," Little Joe replied. "Whar y'all comin' from? And who's that colored man you got with you?"

"Just never you mind, Little Joe," Raider said. "Take care of these mounts for me. Here's a dollar for you."

"Excuse me, Raider," Thomas said. "I should like to introduce myself to this gentleman. Hello, sir. My name is Thomas."

"Glad to know you, Thomas," Little Joe replied.

Thomas handed Little Joe a double eagle.

"*Real* glad to know you, sir," Little Joe added.

"I appreciate you taking care of my horse," Thomas said.

"I'll do a real good job," Little Joe replied.

He hurried to his task. Thomas stood for a moment watching as the little man whisked the saddles off the horses with no effort at all. He was stronger than he looked. Raider was watching too.

"He's the best man with a horse I've ever seen," Raider said.

"Somehow it hurts me to see a man working like that," Thomas replied. "Especially an old man. My father died in the fields."

Raider frowned at Thomas. "Ain't nothin' ever come your way?"

Thomas laughed. "Yes, many things. This whole affair has me off my feed, I'm afraid."

"Come on," Raider said. "Let's go meet Claire. And don't forget your rifle. I ain't plannin' on bein' bushwhacked again."

They trudged up through the mucky yard, tracking thick footprints on the wooden steps. Under a crude porch roof they removed their boots and left them on the porch deck. Raider slowly opened the cedar-planked door, listening for signs of movement in the red-trimmed parlor. When he heard nothing, he slid in quietly. Thomas came in behind him.

"Extraordinary," Thomas said. "The inside looks nothing like the exterior."

"Ole Claire likes to pretend she's a Frenchy," Raider replied.

"Fine satin curtains," Thomas said, fingering the drapes that covered the entrance to the main parlor.

"Too early," Raider said. "Whores don't exactly get up at dawn. Ever'body's asleep."

"Not everybody."

Raider turned toward the staircase that led to the second floor. A thin, lanky woman stood at the top of the stairs, pointing a shotgun at them. A pale, slender finger was wrapped around the trigger. Long brown hair spilled over her left shoulder onto her red satin robe. The imprint of her firm nipples pushed through the tight, shiny fabric. Raider had always thought of Claire as being too skinny.

"Hell, Claire," Raider said. "Ain't nobody but me. And I brung a friend. This is Mr. Thomas. Hell, don't open up on me with that scattergun."

"Damn your hide, Raider," Claire cried. "You scared me

half to death sneakin' in here. You should have knocked. You know I always count my money in the morning."

"Didn't you hear us ride up?" Raider asked.

"Who can hear anything in this rain?" Claire replied. "This storm has got me spooked."

Claire lowered the shotgun and came down the stairs. Her long, slender legs flashed in and out of the robe. Thomas thought her face was pretty. High cheekbones, prominent nose, thick, sultry coral lips. She walked off the staircase and came face to face with Thomas. Her smile was warm.

"Mr. Thomas," she said. "Don't you know better'n to hang around with the likes of Raider?"

"I'm forced to the association by professional necessity," Thomas replied. "He's handling a case for me."

"That right?" she said, nodding dubiously.

"Sure enough," Raider chimed in. "Now, what say you give us a couple of rooms?"

"Yes, we would greatly appreciate the opportunity to sleep," Thomas rejoined.

"My, but he talks real fancy," Claire said. "Maybe he really is your boss, Raider."

She slid in front of the big man from Arkansas. She was tall, almost able to look him in the eye. Raider felt uncomfortable with Claire's slender body so close to him. She lifted the wet Stetson from his head and touched the blood-stained bandage.

"You're hurt," she said softly. "Let me take a look at it."

"How come women always have to look at your ailments?" Raider barked. "Get away and fix us a couple of rooms. And make sure there's hot water in the bathhouse."

Claire made an obscene gesture in Raider's face. "Go stick it up a mule," she said. "Thomas, you want a room?"

"Well, I . . ."

"What the hell?" Raider said.

"Tina!" Claire shouted. "Get out here!"

"What happened?" Raider asked Thomas. "She was goin' along just fine and then she starts screaming."

"Tina!"

But Tina didn't come, so Claire went after her.

"You're a smart man, Thomas," Raider said. "What's the matter?"

"I think Claire is sweet on you, Raider."

"Me?"

"Watch out," Thomas said. "She's after you."

Claire stormed back into the main parlor with Tina behind her. The Chinese girl was stark naked and rubbing the sleep from her almond-shaped eyes. Claire turned her around and paraded her in front of Thomas.

"Look at this, Mr. Thomas," Claire said. "What do you think about Tina? Would you like to have a little bit of this? She's Raider's favorite girl."

"With all due respect," Thomas replied. "I surely would like to have me a little bit of that, Miss Claire."

"Use the room at the top of the stairs," Claire said. "Be good to him, Tina."

The Chinese girl understood her task. She took Thomas's hand and led him up the stairs. Thomas couldn't stop smiling. Raider looked as pitiful as a hound dog who had to stay home while the other dogs went hunting. He was baffled by Claire's irate behavior. If he hadn't been so tired, he would have been angry himself.

"What the hell did I do?" he asked.

Her green eyes were dancing like flames in a bonfire.

"You ain't done nothin'. You ain't never done nothin' to *me*, for instance."

"What?"

"What's wrong with me, Raider?" she asked. "You been comin' here for two years, and you done chose every girl but me? Ain't you never noticed how I smile at you?"

"Well, yeah, I guess I noticed."

"Why ain't you never done nothin' about it?" she accused.

Raider shook his head. "I don't know," he mumbled.

"You've never wanted to fuck me?"

"Not particularly."

"Why not?"

"I guess I always thought we was friends," Raider replied.

"I kinda respect you. I guess I never thought much about it."

She lowered her robe from her shoulders, revealing her soft, tender skin.

"Don't you think I'm pretty?" she asked.

"Yeah, I reckon. You ain't got much meat on you, but you look all right."

Her shoulders fell back into her robe as her voice became angry again.

"I'd break your skull if it wasn't already broken," she cried. "How the hell did you do that anyway?"

"Johnny Denton took a shot at me," he replied.

"The Kid?"

Raider's eyes narrowed. "What do you know about him?" he demanded.

Claire raised the shotgun at him. "Don't come any closer," she said.

He would have grabbed her and shook it out of her if she hadn't been waving the scattergun.

"Tell me what you know about Johnny Denton," Raider barked.

"Why should I tell you?"

"He stole a thousand dollars from me," Raider growled.

"You musta been sleepin'," she replied.

"Aw, hell, you're just shittin' me. You don't know nothin' about the Oklahoma Kid."

"Oh yeah," she replied. "Well maybe I know a lot about the Kid. Maybe I got a girl who sees him regular. And maybe he likes to talk on the pillow. And maybe my girl likes to tell me everything the kid says."

"I oughta—"

"One step closer and you'll have an extra mouth," she threatened. "Course, maybe we could work a deal. Maybe we should go up to my room and talk about it. I got a new tub. I'll give you a bath."

Raider didn't see how he could refuse, even if it was blackmail.

"All right," he said. "You done beat me."

"You won't regret it. I'm gonna do *everything* to you. You'll see. I been wantin' to get my hands on you. All the other girls talk about how big you are. Now I finally get to see it for myself."

"Will you at least put down that scattergun?" Raider asked.

"Anything you say, honey. Oh, Raider. You'll never want another woman when I get through with you. I promise."

He watched as her long legs carried her up the stairs. She didn't look bad from behind. And her face was pretty. Not much of a chest, but that didn't always matter. Raider wondered how he would feel about her after they . . . Damn it all, she was just too skinny!

The printer's name was Harlan Huckleby, originally from Kentucky. He was a thin, sour-looking man who turned out to be much more amiable than his appearace. The printing shop had been open for only eight months, and Huckelby wasn't sure if he was going to stay solvent much longer. Oh, he printed a few wanted posters for the marshal. And once in a while Delmonico's changed their menu. Huckelby supposed he would stay in business as long as people kept breaking the law and eating. Of course, the town was growing, so it might not be long before things picked up.

Doc noted the details of Huckleby's life with a sort of sad reluctance. But he let Huckleby chatter on because a man who liked to talk would be more likely to answer questions—just to keep talking. Doc kept hoping he would talk about the slick gentleman who came into his shop about six months ago and ordered the bills of sale for the Hutchison Western Title Company. However, Huckleby did not mention such a man, so Doc chose a lull in the conversation to confront him with the bill of sale.

"Yep, that's my handiwork," Huckleby said proudly. "I seem to remember printing up about fifty of them. Didn't take long. One of my first jobs out here."

"And the gentleman who purchased these invoices, did he say he would be coming back?" Doc asked.

"Weren't no gentleman who purchased them," Huckleby replied.

"No?"

"Nope, it was a woman," Huckleby said.

"Are you sure?"

"I know a woman when I see one," Huckleby replied. "She was a pretty woman, too."

"Had you seen her in town before?"

"Nope," Huckleby replied. "She just sashayed in here and asked me to print up those bills. I told her I'd have to charge her a dollar apiece, because I wasn't sure I could do the job the way she wanted it. But she plopped down two double eagles and a sawbuck and told me she'd take fifty."

"Do you recall anything unique about her appearance?"

"Do I ever," Huckleby chortled. "I ain't no married man, so I take notice when I see a nice-looking gal coming into my shop. She had curly black hair and brown eyes. She also had a beauty mark on her right cheek. She was kinda dark, too."

"Was she Spanish or Indian?"

"Mighta been either one," Huckleby said. "But she talked just like you and me. Had a pretty voice. Not high like a bird, more like a . . . hell, I don't know."

"Was she young?" Doc asked.

"Well, she wasn't no girl. It's hard to say."

"Did she mention a husband or a brother? Someone she might have been traveling with?"

"Nope," Huckleby replied. "She didn't say nothin' about a husband, but I seem to remember she was married."

"And why do you remember that?" Doc asked patiently.

"I don't rightly know," Huckleby replied.

"Do you have a record of the transaction?" Doc asked.

"Yes, I keep track of everything I do. Learned that from my partner back in Louisville."

"Will you get it for me?" Doc asked.

Huckleby leaned forward in his chair. He was chewing on a toothpick, staring at Doc with cautious eyes. "Reckon I have to ask who you are, mister."

"My name is Weatherbee," Doc replied, unpocketing his credentials. "I'm a Pinkerton operative on assignment in this area. Of course, you don't have to show me your records. I could go to the deputy marshal and we could come back here to see if you have anything to hide from the law."

"Nice printing job on your license," Huckleby said. "I'll show you what you want to see. No need to get huffy."

Doc chided himself for his lack of professional demeanor. He was tired, and Huckleby's tiresome manner wasn't helping any. And where had the woman come from so suddenly? Thomas had not mentioned her at all. Huckleby reached into his desk and produced a box of business records for the year.

"When I take on work, I make them pay a deposit," Huckleby said as he rummaged through the papers. "That way you know they're gonna come back. Make them sign a receipt when they pick it up, too. That way they can't come back and say they never picked it up, you know, try to cheat you by saying they want their deposit back."

"Did you learn that from your partner in Louisville?"

"Hell, I bet I don't have forty receipts for this year. Here they are, Mr. Weatherbee."

Both receipts were signed in a woman's flowing hand. The first signature read "Lorna Pixton." The second receipt, dated a month later, had been signed by Mrs. S. Wolcott. Again the S and W were repeated. He had a woman helping him.

"And the woman placed the order and then called for the finished work?" Doc asked.

"I can still remember her shape," Huckleby replied. "She wasn't fat, but she was, you know, full in all the right places. Since I seen her, ain't a day goes by that I don't think about the way she moved."

She had signed the deposit receipt with her maiden name, Doc thought. Then, in the month that followed, she had married Mr. S. Wolcott. She was married when she picked up the printing. Or she had been married right before she placed the order and had neglected to remember her new name. Another player in the drama.

"Did you print anything else for them?" Doc asked.

"Nope, that was the only order," Huckleby replied.

"Did the woman say where she lived, or where she might be going?"

"Told me she was staying at the hotel," Huckleby replied. "Hell, she paid me in full before I did the job. I didn't have any right to ask her about her business. Did she do something wrong?"

"That remains to be seen," Doc replied. "I can't really disclose the details of my case."

Doc didn't want to tell the printer about the land swindle that had cheated Thomas. Word traveled around too fast. If Mr. S and W was in town, Doc didn't want to scare him off. At any rate, Doc felt better that he was making some progress.

"You've been a great help, Mr. Huckleby," Doc said.

"Glad to be of assistance. Let me know if you need anything printed."

Doc ran back to the hotel through driving sheets of rain. His spats were nearly ruined by the time he stepped into the warmth of the lobby. The desk clerk who had helped him with the register was going off duty. Doc caught him and pulled him into the privacy of a shaded corner.

"Why didn't you tell me about the woman?" Doc asked.

"What woman?" the clerk replied, trembling in his shoes.

"The woman who was with Wolcott."

"Who?"

"I mean the woman who was with Stephen Winston," Doc said.

The clerk pondered a moment. Either he was acting or he was really as dim-witted as he seemed to be. Doc decided that he was not too bright and needed his memory jogged.

"She was a dark woman, with a beauty mark," Doc said. "Shapely. She moved really well, like a lady."

"Yes, I remember her now. Yes, she was with Winston. A pretty woman with a mole on her cheek."

"What was her name?" Doc demanded.

"I never asked."

"Did she celebrate a wedding or anything similar?" Doc asked.

"No, nothing like that. She was only here a few times."

Doc left him standing in the corner. He braved the rain again, slopping through the muck to the marshal's office across the street. The deputy took the better part of an hour to determine that no one named Lorna Pixton had been married in

Dodge City. Nor had Mr. S. Wolcott taken his vows in Kansas. They double-checked with the preacher to make sure—another trek through the mud. Doc would have to buy a new pair of Melton overgaiters.

When pressed, the deputy remembered the woman's appearance. But he didn't know her name or if he had seen her with a man who looked like the man Thomas described. There were no wanted posters on any of the names Doc had discovered. Doc thanked him and headed for the hotel.

Back in his room, Doc sorted it out logically. Mr. S and W, presumably the man who swindled Thomas, was working out of Dodge City with a woman named Lorna Pixton, a woman he had presumably married along the way. Lorna Pixton ordered fifty fake bills of sale from the printer and then picked them up as Mrs. S. Wolcott. She had been seen in the hotel when Stephen Winston was registered. Mr. S and W had also registered twice before as Stephen Winston. It was a logical assumption that all three visits to Dodge City involved the same nefarious business. Perhaps Thomas had not been the first victim of the confidence game.

Doc leaned back on the bed. Outside, huge drops of rain were smashing against the window. Mr. S. Wolcott, alias Wilson Samuels, alias Stephen Winston, was probably no longer in Dodge City. The logical place to start looking for him was New Mexico, where the swindle had taken place. But Doc decided to think about it after he slept. He wanted to be at full strength when he started out on the trail.

Raider lay back on the clean sheets, still warm from the bathwater of Claire's steaming tub. He wanted to sleep, but he knew that Claire wasn't going to let him. She had been hopping around the room like a long, tall whitetail doe. Raider watched her as she stood by the wall, giggling and laughing at something Raider could not see.

"What the hell you doing?" he asked.

"Come here," she replied. "Take a look at this."

"What the hell you lookin' at?"

"I've got a hole in the wall," she replied. "I can see Thomas and Tina going at it. Umm, she's having a good time. Oh my, is he hung!"

"Get away from there, you whore!" Raider cried.

Claire didn't move. She kept on describing what Thomas was doing to the Chinese girl. If she meant to make him horny, she was succeeding. Raider could not fight the stiffening between his legs.

"Oh my goodness," Claire said, turning away from the eyehole. "Thomas is well-built."

She looked at Raider's groin.

"But he ain't got nothin' on you, honey," she cooed.

Her red robe fell to the hardwood floor. Raider took in the slender curves of her white body. Smallish breasts, thin waist, narrow hips, and long legs ending at the brunette wedge between her thighs. He never went in for lean girls, but he had to admit that Claire wasn't bad. She was even kind of classy.

"Disappointed?" she asked.

"Hell, no! Get over here."

"Slowly," she replied. "I'm going to take my time with you. You just lie back and relax."

She slid next to the bed, lowering her fingertips to the curls of hair on his chest. She traced the lines of his muscles and then put her lips on his nipples, kissing and using her tongue in a most professional way. Her curiousity got the better of her when she touched his scars. Raider had to explain how he got them before she would continue with her skilled hands.

"You're starting to like it already, aren't you?" she whispered in his ear. "You'll always come back to me when I get finished. And if you make me happy, I'll tell you everything you want to know about the Oklahoma Kid."

"Get on your back," Raider said.

"Oh no," she replied. "Not before I've had my fun."

She went back to work on him, using her hands and lips, following the line of hair down the middle of his torso, kissing his stomach. Raider's eyes were half shut, and his breathing was starting to get ragged. Claire was in complete control of him. He would have done anything she asked.

"Jesus," Claire said, taking his rigid organ into her petite hands. "I'd heard how big you are, but now I believe it."

"You never watched me through your peephole?" Raider moaned.

She only laughed and gripped his cock like an ax handle. Her curious eyes seemed to examine every fold and line, as if she had never seen the male organ before. Without warning, her tongue came out of her mouth and lapped the swelling head. A shiver went through Raider's body.

"You like it with my mouth," she said, her green eyes full of mischievous lust. "I ain't done it much, but I heard you like it. Want me to do you with my mouth first?"

"Just get on with it," Raider moaned.

As her lips engulfed his manhood, Raider doubted the claim that she had never had much experience with her mouth. Claire tortured him, sliding up and down, cupping his scrotum and kneading his testicles with her expert fingers. Raider wondered if she was going to make him come that way. He held back, vowing to save his discharge for later.

"I bet you're wonderin' if I take it all inside me," Claire said, gazing up at him with her devilish irises. "You think skinny girls are too tight, don't you? We'll just see about that."

She climbed onto the bed with him. Raider tried to grab her to pull her down, but she brushed his hands away. Her lips spread out in a grin that reminded Raider of a treed possum. She straddled his body, pinning him to the bed.

"You ain't gonna have it your way," she teased. "Not just yet, anyway. Umm, it's so damned big."

She had it in her hand, rolling it around like a billy club. Raider watched her as she rubbed the end of his phallus on her wet crotch. Claire had closed her eyes, but she was still smiling that shit-eating grin. Raider thought he might explode right there, but he managed to hold back.

"Here goes," Claire said.

Her smile disappeared as she lowered herself onto his prick. Slowly the entire thick length penetrated her vagina, leaving her to bite her lip with a mixture of pleasure and pain. When she was thoroughly impaled, she started to breath heavily.

"Are you all right?" Raider groaned, feeling his throbbing

shaft inside her, hoping she would never take it out.

Claire sucked in air between her clenched teeth.

"Wait," she moaned. "Wait a minute. Let me get used to it. I need to stretch some and then it will be all right."

She just sat there on top of him, her white thighs rubbing against his own legs. Raider closed his eyes and concentrated on the things she was doing with her female muscles. He had plugged her completely, but she was making the adjustment.

"How does it feel to have it inside me?" Claire asked.

Why did women always have to be told? he wondered.

"It feels good," he managed. "Just shut up and fuck me, damn it. If you been wantin' it for so long, then you're finally gettin' it, so shut your yap."

Claire replied by raising her body a few inches. Then she fell again, impaling herself a second time. It didn't seem to be hurting her anymore. Raider kept his eyes open as she repeated the rise and fall, slowly taking his length in and out of her.

"I do love a big one," Claire moaned through tight lips.

As she increased her motion, she reached back, twirling his scrotum in her hand, squeezing him like a milk cow. She wanted to make him give it up, to show her dominance over him by making him come her way. Raider let her have her head for a moment and then he took charge.

"Let's do it the natural way," he replied, cupping her tight buttocks with his hands.

In a swift motion, he spun her around, rolling with her, keeping his cock inside her. Claire cried out when Raider's body weight pressed her to the sheets. But Raider could tell by the dreamy expression in her eyes that she wasn't hurting. She licked her lips and squirmed on the mattress under him. Her hands came up to grab his shoulders, as if she had wanted to pull him all the way inside her.

"Give it to me," she whispered, wrapping her long legs around his waist. "Hard as you can. Don't worry, I won't break."

Raider was surprised by the supple strength of her body. As his hips began to rise and fall, Claire met every thrust with a thrust of her own. The wetness from her crotch mixed between them, flowing thick with every joust of Raider's lance. Her fingernails dug into his buttocks, spearing him on with a subtle stinging.

"Harder, cowboy," she cried. "Hard as you can."

"Damn you," Raider said. "Are you half mountain lion, woman?"

He stopped for a moment, trying to catch his breath. Fatigue was setting in.

Claire showed no signs of tiring, however. "What's the matter, Pinkerton?" she teased.

"I'll show you."

"Wait," she said. "Let's do something else."

"Like what?"

"I know a few other ways to get that big thing in and out of me," she replied. "Here, get off and let me show you."

She shivered when Raider withdrew from her. Quickly she wriggled out from under him and faced the headboard of the brass bed. Spreading herself for entry from behind. Raider reached up and ran his fingers over the smooth, white skin of her buttocks.

"Ain't I got a nice ass? Come on, cowboy, put it in me. Or ain't you never done it like this?"

Raider positioned himself behind her, poking and prodding blindly with his blunt cock. He almost entered the wrong way before Claire reached back to guide him. She rested the head on her wetness, bracing herself for the penetration.

"I may be good," she moaned, "but I couldn't take that thing up my ass. Not...ooooh..."

Raider drove home the spike like a railroad worker nailing down a track. He expected Claire to stop him, but instead she only arched her back and met each thrust with an opposite motion. The brass bed rattled as they tested each other's stamina. Claire finally let go of the brass rail and collapsed face down in the feather pillow.

"Had enough?" Raider asked.

She responded by bouncing her backside off his cock. He felt his scrotum bumping against her wedge of pubic hair. Claire reached beneath herself and did something with her hand. Raider wondered if she had touched herself somehow. There were just a hell of a lot of things that he didn't know about women.

"I want it," she said. "All of that milk, honey. Give it to me, Raider. Hurry."

Using what was left of his strength and instinct, Raider grabbed her hips, pulling her back on his cock. As he looked down, he could see it going in and out of her pinkness, the thick bulge wrestled between them like a stiff sidewinder. No woman had ever acted with him like Claire was acting. Not as far as he could remember, anyway.

Claire was gulping air like she was having a seizure or a fit. But Raider never let up. He was going to tame her if it took him all night. His relentless hips thrust forward, forcing tremors through Claire's long body. A shiver would start at her hips and then whip up her body like a curl in a rope.

Raider slipped a hand up her stomach, stroking the tight buds of her nipples. Her skin was burning under his touch. The heat was running up his loins, sparking the rise that had subsided earlier. Claire felt the bulging of his prick inside her.

"Here it comes," she groaned. "Oh, cowboy."

Raider made no effort to hold back. He grabbed her hips and sank his prick to the deepest point of her, erupting with a burst that reduced Claire to quivering surrender. She plummeted to the mattress with Raider falling on top of her, keeping the rigid length inside as it drained.

"Don't pull out yet," she gasped.

He lay on her back, letting his prick rest in the warmth of her wet vagina. Claire's hand was still underneath her. Raider wondered if that hand had anything to do with the trembling of her body, the muscular quaking that slowly subsided. He rolled off her finally, withdrawing the source of their pleasure.

"You all right, woman?" he asked, reclining next to her.

She could barely speak. She nodded, snuggling down close to Raider's body, reaching over to hold the limp timber between his thighs. He half expected her to revive him and put him through the same motions again.

"Sleep," she said softly. "Both of us."

"All right," he replied. "But when we wake up, you have to tell me about the Kid."

She nodded again, resting her face on his chest. Raider

stroked the thin lock of hair that had fallen over her forehead. Damn it all if she wasn't something of a tiger, he thought. She didn't seem to be so skinny after all!

CHAPTER FIVE

Raider jumped when he felt the hand stirring him from his deep, dreamless sleep. Claire was standing over the bed with a finger to her lips and the other hand clutching the neck of her robe. Raider shook his head trying to orient himself. Pale light on the crimson bedroom curtains told him he had slept through the night almost until dawn. His brain was groggy and his skull ached. And his ears sure as hell didn't like the worried tone in Claire's voice.

"Get up, Raider," she said. "He's here."

"Who? What the hell are you talkin' about?"

"Billy Simpson," she whispered.

"Don't know him," Raider replied. "Let me sleep some more."

"He rides with the kid, honey—the Oklahoma Kid!"

"Why the hell didn't you say so?"

A pot of hot coffee couldn't have rousted him any faster. The adrenaline coursed through him, obliterating all pain and fatigue. Raider stepped into his pants and then strapped on his holster.

"Where is he?" Raider asked.

"Downstairs, in the back. Raider, promise you won't kill him. My girl, she's crazy in love with him and she—"

"How long's he been here?" he asked.

"About two hours."

"Why didn't you wake me sooner?"

"Because of my girl," she replied. "He just got what you came here after. I wanted them to have some time alone."

"Damned sentimental woman!"

"Raider, you aren't going to kill him, are you?"

"No, I ain't gonna kill him," Raider replied. "I just want

him to tell me where I can find my money. And then he's goin' into town for the marshal to take care of. He'll get a fair trail, same as anybody else."

"That's all she can ask, ain't it?" Claire said. "Hell, I wish his kind wouldn't come here. How come my girls try to fall in love with the worst trash they can find?"

"Nobody ever arrested one of your girls for having too much smarts," Raider replied as he slipped on his boots. "Anybody with Simpson?"

"No, he came alone."

"He must love that chippy somethin' awful," Raider said.

"You think so?"

"He's gotta be in love to do something as stupid as come this close to Dodge after robbin' that train."

Raider slipped on his shirt. He wanted to be ready if Simpson bolted. He didn't know Simpson by reputation at all, but anyone who rode with Johnny Denton had to be quick and mean. He decided against waking Thomas to cover him. Another gun might complicate things. Raider needed Simpson alive.

"Think he'll stay long?" Raider asked.

"I don't know," she replied. "He usually leaves after the roosters start crowing."

"Which door is closest to where he's sleepin'?" he asked.

"The back."

Raider parted the curtains and gazed out into the yard. Claire had a regular farm going—cows, horses, chickens, a garden. Raider was going to admire it as soon as he had a talk with the man downstairs.

"At least the rain's stopped," Raider said.

A rooster crowed outside.

"He's gonna be movin'," Raider said. "Where's the best place to cover the back?"

"How the hell should I know?"

"Shit, there's too much open ground between the house and the stable. Maybe I should—"

A door slammed downstairs. Sounds of shuffled feet and a woman's voice resounded up the staircase. Boots stomped toward the back door through the house. The woman's voice followed the boots. She was calling, "Billy!"

"Goddamn it, why don't nothin' ever work the way I want it to?" Raider muttered.

The roof would be the quickest way to cover Simpson's exit. Raider opened the window and stepped out onto the wooden shingles. The roof grade sloped downward to the back porch. Raider stepped sideways down the incline, his hand filled with his .44. He settled at the crease where the porch roof jutted away from the house. He kept waiting for Billy Simpson to bolt, but the hombre did not appear in the yard.

Beneath him on the porch, Raider heard the scuffling of bodies, the cry of a distraught woman, and then the crisp slap of a hand against someone's face. Then nothing, like he was kissing her goodbye. Raider thumbed back the hammer of the .44.

"Get movin'," Raider mumbled under his breath.

Boots clapped off the wooden steps. Simpson came out into the yard, his slicker circled around his body as he tromped through the soggy ground. Raider stepped onto the porch roof for balance.

"Far enough, Simpson," he shouted.

Raider had never seen anyone as fast as Billy Simpson. As he spun toward Raider, Simpson's slicker hid the speed of his hands as he brought up a sawed-off Remington double-barreled ten-gauge scattergun. Raider dived for the roof, squeezing off a round in Simpson's direction. A wall of buckshot flew over his head. The roof collapsed under Raider's crashing weight and he tumbled down onto Billy Simpson's girl, who had been screaming for her lover to flee. She broke Raider's fall and was stunned herself instead of the big man from Arkansas. Raider scuffled to his feet.

"Thomas!" Raider called. "Muster out with that Henry rifle!"

His .44 had fallen into the mud. As he lifted it from the mire, a horse bolted from the stable with Billy Simpson in the saddle. Raider squeezed off his five remaining rounds at the moving target. Simpson fell from the horse, squirming on the soupy earth.

"Son of a bitch!" Raider said. "I can't believe I hit him."

Simpson's girl lunged off the porch steps onto Raider's

back. She went for his eyes with her fingernails. He managed to grab her wrists to keep her from blinding him. Claire ran up from behind, pulling the girl's hair, trying to dislodge her from Raider's shoulders.

"You shot my Billy! You shit-eatin' dog!"

The three of them tumbled into a puddle, wrestling until they were covered with grime. Claire managed to subdue the hysterical girl, trapping her in a tight bear hug. Raider staggered to his feet, reloading his gun as he walked toward the limp body of Billy Simpson.

"Raider! Look up!"

He turned to see Thomas standing on the roof, his Henry rifle in hand.

"Cover me," Raider called back. "This here's one of Johnny Denton's boys. He might still be kickin', so don't shoot less'n—"

As Raider spoke, Billy Simpson lifted the sawed-off shotgun from the mud. Thomas's rifle precluded any report from the double barrels. Simpson's face had disappeared, smashed into bloody fragments by Thomas's accurate slug.

"Damn it, man, why did you have to kill him?" Raider cried. "Now he can't tell me where to find my money."

The shooting had awakened everyone in the house. Men who had stayed too long ran for their wagons and horses. Raider called Little Joe and told him to hitch up the buckboard. The body would have to be taken into town.

"You afraid to take this dead man into the marshal's office, Little Joe?" Raider asked.

"No, sir, long as he ain't alive."

They rolled up the body of Billy Simpson in an old blanket and put it in the back of the wagon. Raider's stomach was churning. He hated to kill someone or even be a part of it. Especially someone who might have led him to his thousand dollars. He watched until Little Joe was out of sight and then turned back to wave to Thomas, who was still on the roof.

"You mind keepin' an eye out for a while?" he asked.

"Sure enough, Captain," Thomas called back.

When Raider went back into the house, Claire was waiting

for him. She looked damned pretty, he thought, even though her thick mouth was kind of pouty-like. She was mad about something.

"Why did you have to kill him?" she cried. "You told me you wouldn't. I begged you not to."

"I didn't mean to shoot him," Raider replied. "I just got off a lucky shot."

"Not so lucky for my girl!" Claire shouted. "Now she's gonna cry her eyes out, and I'm gonna be short a girl for a week!"

Raider pointed a threatening finger at her.

"Let go of it, woman," he barked. "Now, I'm damned sorry that I had to shoot that boy off his horse. And I'm even sorrier that Thomas had to kill him. But since somebody was gonna die, I'm glad it was Simpson and not me."

"What about my girl?"

"I wouldn't worry too much," Raider replied. "Hell, she'll get over it. And before you know it, she'll up and be in love with some other upstandin' citizen like Billy Simpson."

She drew back a hand to slap him. He caught her wrist and twisted her arm around her back. She squirmed until she saw she couldn't get away.

"You black-eyed bastard!" she cried.

"I'm takin' you upstairs," Raider replied. "And you're gonna tell me ever'thing I need to know about the Oklahoma Kid."

"I ain't never—"

But Raider whisked her upstairs. He knew how to calm her down. After a bath and bed, she told him about the Kid. Raider was preparing to go after Johnny Denton when Little Joe returned from town. The marshal had taken care of getting the body to Boot Hill. Everything was fine, "Ceptin' for one thang," Little Joe told Raider.

"What's wrong now?" Raider asked.

"Gen'tleman called Doc said you s'posed to come to the hotel right away. Said you gonna be in trouble if'n you don't. Said to bring the colored man, too."

"Ain't it just like him," Raider said with a scowl. "Just when I'm ready . . ."

Raider thought about heading out in spite of Doc. He shook his head finally. When he considered facing Doc's wrath, he knew the Oklahoma Kid would have to wait.

Doc sent word to Raider and Thomas because he wanted to meet them in the privacy of his hotel room. A cathouse was no place for a Pinkerton to discuss his findings in a case. And when Doc saw the body of Billy Simpson, he figured that Raider might up to his old tricks, whoring and killing, two things that destroyed Raider's concentration. Losing the poker money to Johnny Denton had put Raider off track. Doc needed all of his partner's skills intact, including Raider's unique abilities to point up any cracks in one of Doc's theories. His mind would work better away from the distractions of the bordello.

Raider and Thomas arrived at the hotel at eight-thirty that morning, an hour after Little Joe had brought word back to Claire's. Doc did not inquire as to the particulars regarding Raider's clash with Billy Simpson. To force a sense of professionalism into the meeting, Doc made Raider take a chair and listen to the evidence and conclusions based on the information gathered in Dodge City.

Mr. S and W, alias Stephen Winston, alias Wilson Samuels, alias S. Wolcott, had been operating around Dodge. On three occasions Stephen Winston had checked into the hotel, perhaps to swindle other hapless settlers. The clerk remembered Stephen Winston, who matched the description given by Thomas. As far as Doc knew, Hutchison Western Title Company was a sham that had been created on the printing press of one Harlan Huckleby. A woman had dealt with the printer, not a man who resembled Wilson Samuels.

"A woman?" Raider asked.

Doc saw that Raider had been listening, thinking.

"Yes, a woman," Doc replied. "Tell me, Mr. Thomas. Did you see a female companion with Wilson Samuels? A well-dressed, mature type, dark with dark hair. Well-turned figure, unforgettable even if you've seen her only once."

"She never appeared during any of my dealings with . . . I don't know what to call him now," Thomas said.

"Samuels for now," Doc replied. "Where did you do business with him?"

"On the trail," Thomas replied. "And then later, on the site in New Mexico."

"How did you hook up with this boy to begin with?" Raider asked. "He just turn up out of the blue?"

"Not exactly," Thomas replied. "We met a man on the trail. He was heading back west, said he had a nice piece of land in New Mexico."

"What was his name?" Doc asked.

"Liam," Thomas replied. "Liam Pixton . . ."

"Pixton!" Doc cried. "That's the very name that appears on the receipt from the printer. Lorna Pixton, the woman I spoke of. Did this Pixton introduce you to Samuels?"

"Not at first," Thomas replied. "We had to convince him that we could really afford to buy property. He said we were crazy to buy land near Dodge City, that Negroes weren't welcomed here. Then he mentioned Samuels, said he would try to find out if there were any more tracts left. Pixton found us a good campsite near a stream. We waited for nearly a week and a half before Samuels showed. He was smooth. He was reluctant to sell to us until we showed him our money. Pixton got him to agree to a meeting at the site of the land. We traveled with Pixton to the New Mexico Territory. Of course, when we saw the land, we purchased it immediately. How could we pass up a chance to have our own spread?"

"You never did business with Pixton in the hotel, then?" Doc asked.

"No."

"What's Pixton look like?" Raider asked.

"Short, gray, balding," Thomas replied. "He's fat, too. I'd say he's fifty, fifty-five years old."

"Sounds like we got more'n one weasel in the henhouse," Raider said. "Sounds like some kind of gang, Doc."

"Including the sheriff who threw Thomas off his land," Doc replied. "It does seem probable."

Raider leaned forward. Doc saw it coming. The critical eye. The unwillingness to believe anything Doc said until it was explained to his satisfaction.

"Just one thing, Doc," Raider said.

"I'm listening."

"Ever'thing you say seems to fit," Raider replied. "The girl's name matchin' the setup man. This dude prancin' around sellin' stuff that the sheriff's gonna take away later. But you only got a bunch of initials and a receipt from a printer. How's that gonna stack up with a judge? It still comes down to the word of a black man against a white man."

"Obviously we need more evidence," Doc replied.

"Or we got to catch this boy at his own game," Raider said. "You got any ideas, Doc?"

"We have to find Wolcott first," Doc replied.

"Wolcott?" Thomas said.

"I believe that to be the culprit's true name," Doc replied. "The woman betrayed him. She signed at the printer with two names, maiden and married. It was important for her to let the world know the second time that she was Mrs. S. Wolcott. I am assuming that our man did not marry her under a pseudonym."

"A what?" Raider asked.

"A false name," Doc replied.

"Do you think Mr. Wolcott is still in Dodge City?" Thomas asked.

"No," Doc replied. "He only uses Dodge City as a place to meet his customers. Pixton is the front man, shilling out unlikely people who are armed with their life savings."

"Seems like a funny place to do business," Raider said.

"Dodge City is quickly becoming a transient center," Doc replied. "Men come in and out, on their way in both directions across the country. The railroad ends here now, but soon the track will go farther west. Even now someone can slip in and out of the area without attracting undue attention."

"It's possible," Raider offered. "Ole Thomas here had to wait for Wolcott to get here. Pixton set him up, sent word to Wolcott. Makes sense."

"Wolcott went in and out of Dodge in one day all three times he came here," Doc replied. "I wonder how many times he's issued those bogus bills of sale."

"You think he really owns that land?" Raider asked.

"Did he show you a deed, Mr. Thomas?" Doc asked.

"Yes, he had a deed," Thomas replied. "An original deed from the homestead. He said he would transfer the deed to our names, but that it would be several months before we got the deed ourselves."

"Looks like we got to find Wolcott," Raider said. "Got any ideas where to look, Doc?"

"Logic dictates that we start looking in New Mexico, near the site of the swindle," Doc replied. "We should also keep our eyes open for other victims of Wolcott's confidence game."

"You think he might be pullin' this shit all over the territory?" Raider asked.

"If he is, we'll certainly put a stop to it," Doc replied.

"I pray you're right," Thomas said.

"Have we overlooked anything, Raider?" Doc asked.

"Maybe we could check at Fort Dodge. See if the army has heard anything about Wolcott."

"They haven't," Doc replied.

The three of them were silent for a moment.

"All things as they are, we shall leave as soon as I can get my wagon from the stable," Doc said. "Is that agreeable?"

Raider glanced up quickly. Doc saw the sudden glint in his black eyes. There might be trouble if Raider was still thinking about going after the Oklahoma Kid and his money.

"Something wrong, Raider?" Thomas asked.

"No," Raider replied, smiling. "Not a danged thing."

Doc wasn't sure about Raider's grin.

"Me and Thomas are ready, Doc. Hell, let's move out!"

When they reached the Santa Fe Trail, Doc found a telegraph wire. He made Raider climb the pole to hook up the telegraph key. Raider waited on the pole until Doc had sent the few particulars to the home office in Chicago: "Making for the border of the New Mexico Territory. Stop. Following leads to find one S. Wolcott. Stop. Advise any knowledge of Wolcott. Stop. Send directions to Santa Fe. Stop." He did not wait for a reply.

For two days on the trail, Raider appeared nervous. He kept

bouncing ahead of them on the bay gelding, his Stetson turning right and left. He also kept bothering Doc for his telescope. He was looking for something, a landmark. Then it occurred to Doc that they were approaching the area where five territorial borders came together. One of those territories was Oklahoma, Johnny Denton's home. Raider was obsessed by his lost fortune once again.

"He's about to do something extremely stupid," Doc said.

"Beg your pardon?" Thomas swung round in the saddle of the chestnut mare and looked at Doc.

"We might lose him shortly," Doc said defeatedly.

Sure enough, Raider's Stetson disappeared on the other side of a ridge ahead. Doc urged Judith on so he might catch up to Raider. Thomas spurred the mare alongside the wagon. But Raider surprised them by riding back over the rise, kicking up dust as the bay flew down the incline. Doc reined Judith and waited for Raider.

"This is it, Doc," Raider said. "There's a little cantina just over that rise. I got to ride south now."

"I won't allow you to go after Johnny Denton," Doc cried.

"You watch me," Raider replied. "He's got my gold, and I aim to get it back if it means takin' his head off."

"This is direct violation of Pinkerton's procedure," Doc said.

"Well, ain't that just a cryin' shame."

"If you set one foot . . ."

"Look, Doc," Raider said. "I know where y'all are headin'. I can catch up. You're gonna be goin' south. You got maybe two more days left on the trail. I'm only riding a half day south of here. I'll meet you in New Mexico. I won't be more than a few hours behind you. What I got to do won't take long."

"What if the home office finds out that you've been conducting personal business on company time?" Doc challenged.

"Then my ass is in the icehouse," Raider replied. "Listen, Doc, you got to respect me on this thing. My honor is on the line. I can't let punks like Johnny Denton push me around. How the hell am I supposed to respect myself?"

Raider knew the honor part would hit Doc close to home. Doc was a sucker for anything noble. Still, Doc wasn't too happy about Raider's leaving, even if he was going to give in.

"Damn you, you Arkansas, river-running, hillbilly bastard!" Doc railed. "Get away from my sight. You have half a day, no more. And if you get yourself killed, don't expect any sympathy or a company funeral. The buzzards can pick your eyes out for all I care."

"You don't swear much, Doc, but when you do, it's a dandy oath. Adios, men. See you in New Mexico."

The gelding's front legs came off the ground. Raider took off his Stetson and waved it over his head. Then the gelding bolted back over the ridge, flying south in a cloud of dust.

"He's an impetuous sort," Thomas said.

"I will never understand why I ended up with such a thick-headed saddle-brained partner," Doc said. "Giddy-ap, Judith."

They went along slowly. Doc needed a cigar. He offered a cheroot to Thomas, who refused. Instead, Thomas took out a small tobacco pouch. He packed a corncob pipe with a crisp green substance. The smoke from his pipe smelled too sweet to Doc.

"An odd aroma from that blend of tobacco," Doc said.

"Not tobacco," Thomas replied, puffing away. "It's an herb used by the Indians. Relaxes the mind and the body. Would you like to try some?"

"Perhaps later."

They ascended the rise and looked south. Raider's trail dust was lingering in the still air. Doc took out his telescope and found a small figure closing in on the horizon.

"He's hell bent," Thomas said.

"He's going to get himself killed," Doc replied. "I hope nothing happens to him."

Thomas laughed. "Y'all are somethin'."

For the first time, Doc heard the true twang of a Louisiana accent in Thomas's deep voice. He had an odd glow in his eyes, and his face was sporting a languid grin. Cannabis in the pipe, Doc thought. He had seen and experienced the effects of the herb himself. Raider called it loco weed.

"Somethin' I can't figure," Thomas said.

"What's that?"

"It's personal."

"Feel free."

"Well, I just can't figure you, Doc. How come a fancy dude like you is out here in the wilderness runnin' around tryin' to solve other people's problems? A gentleman like you could be back in New York or Boston, sippin' tea and havin' your way with the ladies. But you're out here with a crazy white boy workin' for Allan Pinkerton. How come?"

Doc shook his head and laughed.

"I ask myself that question from time to time," he replied. "Oh, I like the parlor and the drawing room well enough. And I certainly prefer Boston to Dodge City. I suppose, ultimately, that civilized society just doesn't present enough challenges for me. One grows complacent on a diet of tea biscuits. And I have the kind of temperment that longs for a problem to solve, the formulaic search for an answer. This occupation provides me the opportunity to do just that."

Thomas just shook his head and kept laughing. The white man in the fancy clothes seemed damned strange to him. Why would anyone want to traipse around the western territories when he could be home in the parlor? Maybe men just had a notion to run away from what was easy. Thomas thought he would have settled for easy—or anything close, for that matter.

According to Claire, Billy Simpson's girl had mentioned a little shack near the Oklahoma-Texas border where Johnny Denton and his gang liked to rest after a job. The location of the shack made it ideal for operating in all five surrounding territories. It was also close to Johnny's mother, Claire said. He liked to see her as often as he could. It was a superstitious ritual with him, especially after a holdup.

To find the shack, a man would have to ride south on the trail for two days, until he reached the Cantina Lorenza. From there it was a half-day's ride to the Oklahoma Kid's private hideout. It was a lonely little slapdash box of boards with a lone stovepipe coming out of the tin roof. And smoke was billowing out the pipe.

Raider did not see the dim glow from the shack until dusk was settling over the plain. He wondered if he would have been able to see the shack without the smoke. It was settled in a low-lying mesquite plain. Raider tied the gelding to a bush and headed for the cabin on foot. He wanted a better look at things before he decided to take action.

In the twilight, Raider counted four horses in front of the shack. Five men, according to Doc, had robbed the train. Thomas had killed two of them. That should have left three, including the Kid. Maybe they had picked up some extra firepower along the way, accounting for the fourth mount.

Raider felt his way through the cool darkness back to his horse. Billy Simpson's sawed-off scattergun was slung over the saddle. He broke it open and dropped two brass cartridges into the chambers. Double-ought buckshot would convince the Kid to give back Raider's gold. Raider took off his Stetson and hung it on the saddle horn. He wanted to move fast, and he didn't want to lose his hat in the bargain. He checked the cylinder of his .44 to make sure all six shots were loaded. Peaceful night sounds were all around him as he started toward the shack.

The men were laughing inside the dilapidated dwelling. Raider kept low in the shadows, trying to circle around to get a better look through the window. He counted four men, but he couldn't tell which one was the Kid. His choices were narrowed. He could wait or take his chances bursting in with both hands full of steel. He had to stay calm.

Sounds of clinking coins set him off. Money was hitting the table, like they were playing poker again. With Raider's double eagles, no doubt. He stood up straight, no longer concerned for his own safety. With the shotgun in his left hand and the .44 in his right, he strode toward the front of the shack. Silently he crept up to the threshold, listening to the laughter and the clinking sound of his money. He took a deep breath and applied his boot to the flimsy door.

"Don't move, boys!"

Two men immediately dived for their guns. Raider caught them with alternate bursts from the barrels of the scattergun. A third man came up with a derringer, but Raider's .44 dispatched him to hell in a heartbeat. Raider expected trouble from the fourth man, but he only had his hands in the air. There was no Johnny Denton.

"Please, señor," the man cried. "Don't shoot me. I am just a Mexican horse trader. I don't know why you come to kill these men, but it is no business of mine."

Raider spun him around in the chair.

"None of these boys ain't Denton," Raider bellowed. "Where the hell is he?"

"Who?"

Raider grabbed the man's shirt and pulled him out of the chair. He dangled at the end of Raider's arm, trembling without resistance. Raider felt a little like a bully, picking on a man so small. But he had to find out the truth.

"Johnny Denton," Raider growled. "He calls himself the Oklahoma Kid. These are his boys."

"Of course, señor, but I am not him. I am Manuel Rojo. Please, you are choking me!"

Raider let him fall back into the chair.

"You was doin' business with these boys," Raider said. "They musta said somethin' about their boss."

"I only sold them horses, señor," Rojo replied.

Raider glanced down at the money on the table. Silver dollars instead of double eagles. His poker winnings were with Denton. When he searched the corpses, he found a few more silver dollars. He turned back to Rojo, who sat wide-eyed in the chair.

"This gun makes a helluva noise and a big hole to boot," Raider said. "How'd you like to find out?"

"No, señor," Rojo replied.

"Then I want some answers," Raider said.

"If I can help you . . ."

"We ain't got time to beat around the bush. You was sellin' these boys some horses. You better tell me what you know, elseways we take a ride into Santa Fe and find out if you're wanted for any horse stealin'."

"Are you the law, señor?"

"Pretty damn close," Raider replied. "Too close if you don't start talkin'."

"What is it you wish to know, señor?"

"Did these boys talk about meetin' the Kid later?" Raider asked.

"Yes, they did. And they call him a mother's boy. You know, like a *maricone*."

"Then he's at his mother's place," Raider said.

"Oh, no. They say he was leaving there soon. And they were going to meet him at another place."

"Where?"

"I don't know for sure. Southwest of here I think. Arizona or New Mexico. Just southwest."

Raider put the .44 in his face.

"You wouldn't be lyin' to me just to save your own hide?" he demanded.

"Oh, no, señor. If you had not killed these hombres, they would have told you the same."

"He's gonna be mighty surprised when none of these boys show up," Raider said.

"Sí, señor," Rojo replied with a laugh.

Raider gathered the money on the table and put it in a pile. With what he had taken from the bodies, he had nearly fifty dollars. Not even close to the thousand the Kid had stolen from him. He felt kind of bad, killing three men for so little.

"What was you gonna charge them for your horses?" Raider asked.

"Ten dollars each," Rojo replied.

"For them nags outside?"

"No, señor, I have remuda about a mile from here," Rojo said. "My brother is with them. I was to signal him when I had the money. One cannot be too careful with men of this sort."

"What kind of signal?" Raider asked.

"A gunshot."

"Then he's probably on the way."

"He is here, señor. Drop the *pistola*."

Rojo's brother was standing at the window, holding an old Springfield percussion rifle. He only had one shot. Raider considered spinning around to drop him, but the angle was bad, and Rojo's brother might get lucky with his one slug.

"Thank you, Pablo," Rojo said.

Raider dropped the .44 into Rojo's open hand. Rojo backed off and motioned for his brother to enter the shack. All this killing and Raider still didn't have the Kid. And now he had let two Mexican horse traders get the drop on him.

"Look here," he said. "I ain't got no truck with you two. These boys took somethin' of mine, and I aim to get it back."

"I will kill him, Manuel."

"No, brother," Rojo replied. "Put down the rifle. This gringo is an important man. We will be in trouble if we kill him."

Rojo held out the .44 to Raider.

"What the hell?" Raider said.

"Take back your gun," Rojo said. "Go on, I am trusting you not to kill us."

Raider took the .44 and slipped it back into his holster.

"What the hell are you up to?" Raider asked.

"A bargain," Rojo said. "You take the silver with you. I will keep the horses and the dead men."

"But, brother—"

"Quiet, Pablo. This hombre will agree. He has no use for these men, and the reward is worth more than all of the silver on the table. Am I right, señor gringo?"

Raider laughed. "Hell, I reckon you're a lot smarter than I thought," he replied. "Okay, Rojo. You got a deal. You say the Kid was heading southwest?"

"Sí, señor. To Arizona or New Mexico. I cannot remember which. These dead men talked about both places."

"I hope it's New Mexico," Raider said, scooping the silver into his pockets.

"Good luck to you, gringo. May the blessed Virgin walk in your footsteps behind you."

Rojo turned to his brother and spoke in Spanish. Together they began to lift the bodies, carrying them to the horses outside. Raider shook his head and laughed to himself. Rojo and his brother were going to look like heroes when they came riding into the nearest marshal's office with the Denton gang dead as doornails.

Raider thought about helping them with the bodies, but he decided that he didn't have the time. He knew he would have to ride hard all night if he was going to rendezvous with Doc and Thomas the next day. He had broken his back for fifty dollars. And it looked like the damned Kid had slipped through his fingers for good.

Doc and Thomas kept a steady pace on the trail the next day. The spring sun was warm, so they rested at midday, keeping an eye out for Raider's entrance. Thomas had shot a prairie chicken that morning, and it served well for their lunch. Doc watched the way Thomas turned the bird on a stick over the coals. The meat was tender and a little gamy.

When the sun began to ease into afternoon, they slipped back onto the trail, heading southwest again. The landscape was slowly changing as they drew closer to the border of New Mexico. Mountains were barely visible on the horizon, and the plain had become more hilly and grassy.

"The Great Plains start here," Thomas said. "They sweep south into Texas."

"How much farther do we have to go?" Doc asked.

"We'll reach my family's camp by tomorrow afternoon," Thomas replied. "Providing that we get an early start in the morning. We've got about two hours of light. About three miles ahead there's a stream where we can camp."

"Good. I could use a bath."

They plodded along in a grassy vale that lay between two small hills. Suddenly Thomas began to glance over his shoulder every couple of seconds. At first Doc thought he was looking for Raider. Thomas was quiet and apprehensive as he reined his mare.

"What is it?"

"Somebody is dogging our trail," Thomas replied.

"How many?" Doc asked.

"Sounds like one person," Thomas replied. "I've been hearing him for about a half hour. I thought maybe he was just . . . shh, there it is again."

"I don't hear anything," Doc said.

"Of course not," Thomas replied. "It's an Indian. I hope it isn't a scout for a renegade party."

"Renegades?"

"Nobody else would be around these parts. At least no other

Indians. Stay on the trail, Doc. Just keep going, I'm going to ride on ahead."

Before Doc could protest, Thomas spurred the mare forward. He disappeared around a bend, leaving Doc by himself. Doc checked the .38 Diamondback in his coat pocket, hoping he would not have to use it. For several long minutes, Judith clomped slowly along the trail. Then Doc heard screaming, like an Indian war cry.

The whip urged Judith to go faster. Doc rounded the bend with his .38 in hand. He looked up to see Thomas riding down the slope. Slung over the saddle in front of him was a live body. When they were close enough, Doc saw that Thomas had captured an Indian girl. Doc could smell her when he brought the wagon alongside the mare. With her scraggly hair and pungent buckskin shift, she looked like the devil's own daughter. She was kicking and screeching, trying to escape from Thomas's grip.

"You've found a friend, I see," Doc said.

"She was following us on foot," Thomas replied. "Look, she isn't even wearing moccasins."

"What tribe would you say?" Doc asked.

"Navajo, probably. But she's too far north to be part of a hunting party."

Thomas spoke suddenly in a harsh language that Doc did not understand. The girl replied in a similar tongue. Thomas laughed.

"She's Navajo, all right," he said. "She came north when her tribe banished her for being a witch. She had trouble with the medicine man. She's been out here a month."

"A tribute to her survival instincts," Doc replied. "Ask her why she was following us."

Again they vocalized in the strange sounds.

"She's wanting to know if we need a squaw," Thomas said.

"Do you believe her?"

"She might have been planning to cut our throats tonight. It's a good thing I heard her."

"I wonder if there's anything we can do about that awful smell," Doc said.

"Let's hurry on and make camp," Thomas said. "We can let her go in the morning."

They picked up the pace and arrived at the stream within the hour. Doc and Thomas both wanted to bathe, so they tied the girl in the back of the wagon. Then they hurried to the stream, disrobing to utilize the last rays of light. Doc waded into the stream with a bar of soap. Thomas followed, but before either one of them could work up a lather, the girl came over the side of the wagon.

"She got out of those ropes!" Thomas cried. "Hurry, before she gets to the guns."

But the girl did not go after their weapons. Instead, she came to the edge of the stream and dropped her buckskin garment. Before either of them could move, she waded naked into the water.

"Look here," Doc said. "You can't do this."

The girl lowered her body into the stream, pulling herself along the streambed until she was next to Thomas. She reached up and touched his head, running her hands over his hair. She kept repeating one word over and over.

"What's she saying?" Doc asked.

"Buffalo," Thomas replied.

"What?"

"It's my hair," Thomas said. "It reminds her of the buffalo's mane. Indians believe that colored men are bison who were turned into men by the Great Spirit."

"Interesting," Doc replied.

"To her, I am a buffalo man. When I wore my uniform, I was the buffalo soldier. I always liked that title for some damned reason."

"Does she have a name?" Doc asked.

Thomas asked her in the Navajo language.

"The tribe called her Girl Who Casts Walking Stick Shadow," Thomas said finally. "And look at her, she is a skinny little thing. She needs some good food to put the meat back on her bones."

"I wonder how old she is," Doc said.

The girl grabbed Thomas's cock under the water.

"Old enough," Thomas said.

He started to use the soap on her, cleansing away the layers of grime. Underneath the dirt, her skin was soft and smooth. Thomas could not resist touching her in certain places. She did not seem to mind at all.

"What shall we call her?" Doc asked. "Her name is too long to bear repeating."

"What about Shadow?" Thomas replied.

"Done," Doc said. "I'll go to the wagon to see if I have something for her to wear. I may have a . . ."

Doc was somewhat shocked when he looked over at them. The girl was straddled over Thomas's crotch, trying to guide his cock into her. Thomas did not seem to be resisting. Doc hurried out of the water, leaving them to their devices, heading back to the wagon to see if he had something that Shadow could wear.

CHAPTER SIX

Doc awoke stiff-jointed and aching in the back of the Studebaker wagon. The wagon floor was better than sleeping on the
ground, but it was still no substitute for a feather mattress. Doc
would have settled for the lumpy hotel bed in Dodge City.
Even a few days on the trail made him long for the comforts
and refinements of civilization.

Sitting up, he stretched his arms and took several deep
breaths, working out the kinks in his wiry body. It was a fine
spring daybreak on the green and promising New Mexico plain.
Fluttering ptarmigan, plump as Rhode Island chickens, flew
over the blossom-dotted ripples of blue grama grasses. They
had camped the night before on a rise above the stream, a good
vantage point for Doc's spyglass. After Doc had stepped into
his shoes and pants, he gave the plain a quick look with the
telescope, hoping to see Raider's gelding on the horizon. But
the only movement was a herd of mule deer that watered a
mile or so away on the northern bend of the stream.

Doc hoped that Raider wasn't lying somewhere with a bullet
in him. He shook his head and strode back to the wagon.
Thomas and the girl were still asleep—in the same bedroll.
Doc wondered how much trouble she might cause. He decided
to think about it after he shaved. The frothy stream beckoned
him down the incline to the rocky bank.

Doc lathered his face and then worked a straight razor over
his whiskers, watching his skilled touch in the circle of a tiny
mirror. His hand moved slowly, section by section, until his
face was shining. Cupping his palms together, Doc splashed
cold water all over his head. Then he went back to the mirror

to comb his hair. When he was as neat as a fresh Cambridge gentleman, he started back up the incline, immediately catching the sweet smell on the air.

In camp, the Navajo girl had risen. She was hovered over a fire, tending Doc's frying pan. While Doc had been grooming himself, the girl had been through his wagon, finding the meal, some sugar, and a jar of molasses. Her tiny hands had fashioned three flat cakes that simmered in the bottom of the pan. Thomas was nowhere in sight.

"Excuse me, miss," Doc said. "Where did he go? Thomas? The other gentleman . . . er, buffalo man?"

The girl looked up at him. Her eyes were the largest part of her oval face. The brown irises had recorded things Doc hoped he would never have to see. Apparently Thomas had given her a red ribbon, which she had tied around her head like a bandanna. Her hair was shining in the morning sun. Thomas had cleaned her up nicely. The only thing that spoiled her appearance was the smelly buckskin shift; without it she might have looked quite pretty.

"Do you understand a word I say?" Doc asked. "No, I didn't think you did. I wonder if you will understand a calico dress? You are a woman, after all. I have a dress in my wagon. I use it for disguises. Raider wore it once in a scheme that didn't work too well. He said he'd shoot me dead if I mentioned it again, but I don't suppose you're going to tell anyone."

The girl looked back down at the pan.

"No, of course, you're not going to tell a soul."

Doc fetched the calico dress and gave it to her. She gasped and cried out when she saw it. No doubt it was the finest thing the poor creature had ever seen. She rubbed the soft fabric against her cheek, making savage noises in the back of her throat.

"Dear girl, don't have a conniption fit," Doc said. "Go behind the wagon and try it on. . . . I say!"

The buckskin hit the ground in a flash. For a moment she was completely naked in front of Doc, who did not avert his eyes. Her breasts were quite small but well rounded. Dark pubic wedge and slight hips. She pulled the dress onto her shoulders. It was too large for her, but she didn't seem to lose her girlish enthusiasm.

"We don't have a seamstress handy," Doc said. "But I suppose it will have to do."

She grabbed Doc's hand and pressed it to her cheek.

"No!" Doc said, drawing away. "That won't be necessary."

She might have done anything if he had been willing to take advantage of the situation. But Doc returned to the wagon, finishing his ritual of dressing for the day. As he buttoned his spats, a loud rifle shot rolled over the rise. The girl stood up and looked north. Doc listened for a moment. A second shot resounded over the plain. The rifle had sounded like Thomas's .44-.40. Doc had heard it before during the train robbery when Thomas had shot one of the thieves. In any case, Doc checked his .38 Diamondback, making sure it was in his coat pocket as he rustled up a pot of coffee.

"Don't worry," Doc said to the fretful girl. "I couldn't see him in my telescope, but I'm sure that Mr. Thomas is shooting something. Given his penchant for hunting, I mean."

True to Doc's word, Thomas came up the rise within ten minutes. The skinned carcass of a small mule deer was slung across the back of his chestnut mare. The girl pulled the pan off the fire and ran to meet him. Thomas gave her a knife, and she immediately went to work on the carcass, stripping out the haunches for dried meat.

"Looks like Shadow made some fry bread," Thomas said as he strode toward the fire. "Navajo food."

"She went through my wagon," Doc replied. "I'm not sure, but I think we're supposed to eat them with molasses."

"That would do nicely," Thomas replied.

He scooped the tortilla-shaped fry bread out of the frying pan, soaking it in thick molasses before he ate. Doc followed, finding the taste rather bland. His hunger was satisfied, however, and he washed the whole thing down with a cup of strong coffee. Thomas also drank the steaming liquid from a tin cup.

"Did you give her the dress?" Thomas said.

"Yes," Doc replied.

"I'll pay you for it," Thomas said.

Doc saw the way Thomas looked at the girl—like a man who was not familiar with love.

"You don't have to pay me for it," Doc replied. "She can wear it when she goes."

Thomas glared at Doc. It was the first sign of anger Doc had seen in the black man. The girl was going to be trouble.

"She isn't leaving," Thomas said.

"We have to let her go," Doc replied. "She can't stay with us. Her presence will only complicate the investigation."

"She's staying with me," Thomas replied bluntly. "I'm going to keep her for my squaw."

"I don't think it wise—"

"That's right, mister!" Thomas bellowed. "You don't think anything about me and that girl there. Shadow hasn't anyplace to go, and I intend to keep her with me."

"Well, if you're certain about this . . ."

Doc stayed calm, trying to steer Thomas back toward a rational mood. Thomas glanced into the fire and then at the girl. A woman could do wicked things to the best of men.

After a bit Thomas seemed to soften. "I am sorry I spoke to you in that manner," he said finally. "But I intend to have this girl with me. I've never had a regular woman since my girl was taken from me on the plantation. Shadow is here for a reason. If it means your dropping my case . . ."

"No, I won't drop the case. But I think you might exercise some better judgment in this. Women have a way—"

Shadow cried out. She and risen from the carcass and was pointing toward the stream. Doc and Thomas turned to see Raider standing a few feet away. His hand held the .44, and it was pointed toward them.

"Y'all are gettin' kinda careless, ain't you?" Raider said, holstering the .44. "Good thing I ain't a varmint. I snuck up on you, and I wasn't even trying."

He saw Shadow over the mule deer.

"Looks like things got interestin' after I left," he said.

"You see," Doc said to Thomas. "She's causing trouble already. While you and I were arguing, someone could have slipped up and shot both of us."

"I don't care!" Thomas shouted back.

"Whoa," Raider said, stepping between them. "What the hell is goin' on here? Y'all are goin' at each other like a grizzly and a wolverine."

"We found that girl yesterday," Doc replied. "She was wan-

dering on the plain by herself. Apparently her tribe threw her
out for being a witch. Mr. Thomas has . . . become quite friendly
with her, and now he wants to keep her as his squaw."

Raider knelt and poured himself a cup of coffee.

"Squaw, huh?" he said, sipping and smiling. "She Apache?"

"Navajo," Thomas replied.

"Navajo squaws ain't as mean as Apache," Raider said.
"You might wake up with a rock in your skull anyways. Course,
you treat her right and she'll do anything you say."

Raider winked at Thomas.

"You mean you don't mind if I keep her?" Thomas asked.

"It's your necktie party," Raider replied.

Doc shook his head.

"I can't fight you both," he said. "Let's get moving."

"She ain't gonna get in the way, Doc," Raider said. "We
just make sure she ain't around when things get rough. Hell,
if ole Thomas there wants a squaw, we can't stop him."

Doc only grunted and stomped over to his wagon. He led
Judith down the incline toward the stream. Raider had never
seen him so huffy over a woman's presence. Maybe it was
superstition. Even Doc got the spooks sometimes. Maybe he
thought the squaw was bad luck.

"Thank you for pleading my case," Thomas said.

"Well, I ain't as touchy as Doc about these things," Raider
said. "Just one thing. If it comes down to us or her, I'm gonna
watch my own tail. Got it?"

"Yes, I got it."

"Good," Raider said. "Now lets go find out if we can get
your land back for you, Mr. Thomas."

"I'm most agreeable," he said, smiling. "Most agreeable."

At noon they turned dead south, leaving the Santa Fe Trail
behind them. According to Thomas, the only way to get to the
site of the land swindle was to cross open territory. His family
was waiting there, he said, and hopefully his younger brother
had been able to feed the two women—his sister and his sister-
in-law. Raider rode close to Doc's wagon, thinking of a way
to spur Doc out of his temper. Before he could say a word,
Doc sat up in his seat and looked out over the plain.

"Listen," he said.

Raider turned his ears to the wind but didn't hear a thing.

"I hear it too," Thomas called back. "Like music."

Raider strained and finally heard the stinging melody of hammer on steel. The railroad! Had it really come that far? Doc turned toward the sound.

"Where are you going?" Raider said.

"To find those hammers," Doc replied.

"Whoa," Raider called. "We ain't got time—"

"It won't take long," Doc said. "Besides, I've got to find out something that's been bothering me."

Raider pulled up alongside him. Thomas shifted his path and followed them, the girl snuggled behind him. Shadow had become a full member of the party.

"What you got in mind, Doc?" Raider asked.

"Something that has been on my mind for some time now," Doc said. "Our swindler, Wolcott if you will, seems to be rather greedy."

"How's that?" Raider asked, glad to have Doc back on the case.

"What if he's not happy to sell a parcel of land that he may or may not own?" Doc said. "Assuming he preys on little people who may fall through the web of territorial justice, he may have sold the land more than once. What if he's pressing his luck for a bigger gamble?"

"You sayin' the land ain't the only pig in the poke?"

"Perhaps," Doc replied, torching the end of a cheroot. "And what bigger poke than the railroad?"

"Let's ride," Raider said.

They hurried toward the new tracks at a steady clip. The terrain had become more hilly, with the Great Plains giving way to a rolling grassland. Behind a knoll of blue grama stood the railroad crew. Raider warned everyone to approach slowly. Sometimes strangers could make a crew jumpy.

A suspicious, bald-headed man came forward to meet them. He was taller than Raider and heavier. His corded arms strained the fabric of his shirt. With his thumbs tucked in his suspenders he looked up at the three men and the girl.

"Y'all bringin' this darkie to work?" the man asked.

"Who the hell are you to call me a darkie?" Thomas barked.

"The goddamn foreman," the bald man replied. "If you're gonna be working for me, boy, I'm gonna have to teach you respect."

"Easy there," Raider said with a smile. "Don't let's get off on a busted bridge here."

"If you ain't gonna give me this nigger," the foreman said, his fat forehead wrinkled over his squinty eyes, "then you must have other bi'ness."

"I'll show you 'nigger,'" Thomas said, springing from his saddle.

Raider thought he was crazy going after the big man like that. Thomas never landed one punch. The foreman swung a haymaker that lifted Thomas off the ground and laid him out cold. Doc and Shadow tended the unconscious black man, dragging him under the wagon.

"You got a right good hammer there," Raider said.

"Don't get that hand too close to that .44," the foreman said. "I got two men covering me from the tracks."

Raider glanced toward the supply car that sat on the iron rail. Two men on top sported rifles. The rest of the crew had stopped working. Most of them were Chinese, a few were European, and the rest were black. Raider smiled at the foreman.

"Look here," he said. "No need to have hard feelings. We're Pinkertons. We'd like to ask you a few questions."

"You ain't askin' nothin', greenhorn," the foreman bellowed. "You and that dandy better clear outta here. Otherwise you might just get your gut busted."

Raider's stomach was churning as he shifted in his saddle. He felt a fight brewing, like the foreman was just the kind of man who didn't want to stop once he got to swinging. Raider didn't feel like matching him blow for blow, so he tried to talk like Doc.

"Now, we're just followin' procedure here," Raider said. "We're on a case, and we'd appreciate you—"

"I said clear out."

Doc rose up from Thomas's prostrate figure.

"Look here, ruffian," Doc said. "You had cause to hit Thomas here. He attacked you, although you provoked him, so you had a right to defend yourself. However, you have no right to send us off without aiding our investigation. I'll have you know that our organization has helped this railroad to recover—"

The big man jerked the lapels of Doc's coat. Doc quickly grabbed his wrist, applying pressure to a sensitive point between the hand and arm. The foreman loosened his grip. He swung again at Doc, who sidestepped the blow. The foreman looked around like Doc had disappeared.

"I'm gonna take you apart," the foreman cried.

He rushed Doc, who shifted his body weight, avoiding the foreman's superior power. Raider watched, keeping his hand close to his side, knowing that Doc would have to use every one of his self-defense tricks. Raider preferred a good right hand to all of those oriental moves, but Doc seemed to do all right with them.

"Wear him out, Doc," Raider urged.

The foreman circled Doc like a baited grizzly bear. Doc studied the brute in front of him, shifting his weight back and forth on the balls of his feet, keeping his balance and distance. The attacker's tilt and posture alerted his keen eyes as to the nature and direction of the oncoming blow. Doc managed to be an inch away from each awkward swing.

"Use your feet," Raider called. "Hell, it's fair—he's twice as big as you."

Doc avoided a lunge and came back up with a side kick that caught the foreman in his muscled breadbasket. The monster only grunted and came on stronger. He chased Doc up and down, swinging and missing, taking Doc's best kicks and staying on his feet. He stopped and wiped the sweat off his forehead.

"Had enough?" Doc asked, hardly out of breath.

"You ain't shit, little man," the foreman bellowed. "Somebody throw me a crowbar."

A piece of steel landed at the foreman's feet. He picked up the bar and came at Doc again. Doc utilized his superior speed, ducking the man until he was exhausted. Raider sat in his saddle, laughing and shaking his head. The foreman turned his attention to the black-haired man from Arkansas.

"The little runt likes to run," the foreman said. "How about you, cowboy? You chicken shit?"

Raider came down out of the saddle.

"Why don't you just tell us what we want to know?" Raider asked. "Wouldn't that be a hell of a lot easier?"

"You Pinkertons ain't nothin' but cowards!"

Raider looked him in the eyes and snarled. "Can't nobody say nothin' about the Pinkertons. You take that back, baldy."

"Eat shit, Pinkerton asshole."

"Tell the boys with the rifles that I'm takin' off my gun," Raider said.

The foreman raised his arm and Raider dropped his holster.

"Toe to toe," the foreman said with a wicked smile.

"Draw the mark, baldy."

The foreman scratched a line with his foot. Raider looked down and put his toe on the mark. Before he could look up, he felt the knuckles on his jaw. He tumbled backward, hitting the ground with a thud. His jaw hurt, but he didn't go out. He had been hit harder. Maybe Doc had taken something out of the big man.

"Get up, Pinkerton," the foreman said. "Let me show you how a real man fights."

Raider jumped up and put his foot on the mark again. The foreman swung, but Raider saw it coming. He dodged the punch and swung low, catching the foreman in the ribs with a counterpunch hook from his left. He brought the hook up again, slamming knuckles into the soft skin of the foreman's temple. The foreman staggered, but he didn't collapse; he cried out and leapt forward, trying to wrap Raider in his thick arms. Raider dropped away from the bear hug and put a heel into the foreman's groin.

"Again!" Doc cried.

Raider hammered the stunned foreman between the eyes. The bald man staggered backward. Doc stuck out a leg and tripped him. He tumbled down, disturbing the dust with his thudding body.

"I thought he was never going down," Raider said.

"Careful," Doc replied. "He may not be through."

The crew had grown restless watching their foreman take a

licking. All fifty of them had sixteen-pound hammers or crow-bars. A few had started forward to help their fallen boss. The man on the ground slowly came to his feet. Relentlessly he stumbled after Raider, only to find his blows falling short. Raider continued to pummel him with rights and lefts, almost hitting him at will. Raider had to respect him for his gumption.

Thomas came to his senses in time to see Raider's knuckles cutting into the foreman's bloody face. Raider was starting to feel bad about hitting him. He backed off and watched as the crew started to swell toward them. They came up behind their boss, wielding their tools as weapons. The bloodied foreman heard them and raised an arm to halt their path.

"Call off your men," Raider said. "We'll clear out."

The foreman swayed back and forth, his face as red as a clay river. Suddenly he started to laugh. His men didn't think anything was funny, however. Raider measured the distance to his gun, but even if he reached it, he could never shoot them all.

"No need to pick up that shootin' iron," the foreman said. "You done whupped me fair and square. You men get back to work."

The crew lingered for a moment, as if some of them were considering an attack on their own.

"I said scatter!" the foreman shouted.

Slowly they went back toward the tracks. Doc started for the wagon. Thomas was on his feet, helped by Shadow. Raider stood looking at the bald man.

"You're a brave honcho," Raider said. "I guess we'll be clearing out now. No hard feelings."

The foreman laughed again.

"I reckon I owe you men a drink," he said. "The name's Rafferty. And I'd be proud to call you both friends and shake your hands."

He extended his calloused paw. That was the funny thing about a big man who liked to fight, Raider thought. If he beat you, he'd treat you like a dog for the rest of your life if you took it. But if you whipped him, it made him respect you, like both of you were brothers or something. One minute he was trying to cave in your skull, the next minute he was pouring good rye whiskey for you in a shady railroad car. . . .

• • •

"So you think this man's swindlin' people has somethin' to do with the railroad?" Rafferty asked as he rubbed whiskey on his split lip. He, Doc, and Raider were sitting in the supply car with glasses in hand.

"No, not at all," Doc replied. "Not directly, anyway. But there might be some connection with the railroad's route and the piece of land involved. Right now I'm purely speculating."

"How do you want me to help?" Rafferty asked.

Raider thought his battered face looked like a rotten Georgia peach.

"I want to look at your maps," Doc replied. "I'd like to compare the route of the railroad with the location of the land in question."

Rafferty focused his blackened, skeptical eye.

"Ain't nobody s'posed to see the maps," he replied.

"Good heavens, man," Doc rejoined. "I've showed you our credentials. If you can't trust *us* . . . why, we're practically employees of the railroad."

Rafferty touched a tender muscle in his stomach. Raider wondered if they had cracked any ribs. The big foreman took a long drink of the rye and then slammed his glass down.

"Two things," Rafferty said. "First, only you get to look at the map, Weatherbee."

"Agreed," Doc replied. "I can get the readings from Thomas on the site of the property. Raider, go out and ask him to write them down for me."

Rafferty had not let Thomas come into the car with them. Company policy did not permit Negroes or Orientals in the supply car. According to Rafferty, they couldn't be trusted. Raider went out to the wagon, where Thomas waited with Shadow.

"Now, the second stipulation," Doc said.

Rafferty poured himself another drink.

"You can't tell nobody about the beatin' you give me," Rafferty replied. "It's bad enough that the crew saw me get it. I'll have to knock a few heads just to show them I'm still boss."

"Done," Doc replied.

Raider came back into the car with the information Doc had requested. Rafferty spread out the maps, and Doc made his calculations. He was finished in five minutes. Raider saw the disappointment in his face.

"Somethin' don't figure, Doc?" he asked.

"The railroad takes a direct western trail just a few miles south of here," Doc replied. "According to the coordinates given to me by Thomas, the land in question is at leasty forty miles away from the line of the tracks."

"That's no good?" Rafferty asked as he rolled up the map.

"Not for what I was thinking," Doc replied. "I thought our man might be using the land to raise capital for another project. But if the land is forty miles away from the nearest tracks, then I doubt if the bigger gamble is connected to the railroad."

"Maybe he's gonna raise cattle and ship them to market," Raider said. "There's a lot of talk about that."

"Has been ever since the railroad come south," Rafferty offered.

"So far we have no evidence to make me believe that Wolcott is involved in cattle," Doc replied.

"Wolcott?" Rafferty said.

"Ever hear of him?" Raider asked.

The bruised foreman shook his head.

"The railroad will run directly into Santa Fe," Doc said.

"That's right," Rafferty rejoined. "Plan to be there next year. Puttin' it down faster than we thought we could."

"So the railroad's arrival would better benefit someone with holdings in Santa Fe," Doc said.

"You think our man is operatin' out of Santa Fe?" Raider asked.

"Put it on the itinerary," Doc replied. "We're probably going to end up there sooner or later." He lifted his glass to Rafferty. "Thank you, sir. You've been helpful, despite our earlier differences."

Raider was rubbing his tender jaw. "Doc," he said. "You think this land could have anything to do with the Santa Fe Trail?"

"It's too far south," Doc replied.

"That don't make any difference," Rafferty said.

"How's that?" Raider asked.

"Once this railroad goes through, the trail's gonna die," Rafferty replied. "Ain't nobody gonna make that trip no more."

"That's bull," Raider said.

"Did y'all take the trail from Independence?" he asked.

Raider shook his head. "No, we took the train."

"I'm telling you, the trail is gonna die," Rafferty insisted.

Doc thought it was the most intelligent thing he had heard the big man say.

"You're welcome to bunk with us for the night," Rafferty offered.

"No, thank you," Doc said. "I believe we will arrive at our destination before tomorrow morning. We've traveled at night before, haven't we, Raider?"

Raider nodded. He could see the look in Doc's eye. Doc was ready to nail down the facts. And the only way to do that was to get moving.

CHAPTER SEVEN

As they ascended an arid ridge and looked down on a natural basin of flourishing grasses, it became immediately apparent why Thomas had been so eager to purchase the land. Rising above the acreage were the Sangre de Cristo Mountains, an arrangement of moderate, craggy peaks that supplied water runoff for the colorful patches of Apache plume and rabbit brush. Doc extended his telescope and followed the line of seven peaks that diminished in size to the southwest. A thick forest area of juniper trees went halfway up the side of a gradual southern slope. It was an ideal place to start a new life.

"Pretty country, ain't it?" Raider said. "God's country."

"How much of this basin was supposed to have been yours?" Doc asked.

"All of it," Thomas replied.

Doc dropped the spyglass from his eye. "There must be a hundred thousand acres here," he said.

"Ninety thousand in all," Thomas replied.

"You told us you only purchased a hundred acres!"

"I didn't want to explain how I got my hands on so much land. It wasn't the sheriff who tore off the other half of the bill of sale, it was me. I was also ashamed for anyone to know that I was swindled out of so much money."

"Red Wolf musta had a bunch of gold," Raider said. "How much did you give for this?"

"A quarter an acre," Thomas replied. "Below homesteader's price."

"That's still over twenty thousand dollars," Doc said.

"Well, like Raider said, Red Wolf had a bunch of gold. And now most of it belongs to a man named Winston, or Wilson, or Wolcott."

"Maybe not for long," Raider said. "Where you got your people hidden, Thomas?"

Thomas pointed toward the juniper forest.

"You got 'em in the trees?" Raider asked.

"No," Thomas replied. "Come on. I have to show you."

A chill persisted in the morning air, making Raider wish he had his heavy wool coat. The sun had only been up an hour, and it still hadn't warmed things up. There was also a bank of dark clouds to the northwest, behind the mountains. More rain maybe. He followed Doc and Thomas into the flat land of the basin.

"I wonder if this Wolcott hombre really owns all of this land," Raider said.

"That's easy enough to find out," Doc replied. "Providing that our path runs into Santa Fe and the territorial records are good."

As they plodded over the basin's springy turf, Raider kept an eye in all directions. He still had Billy Simpson's scattergun on his saddle, just in case an ambush was waiting in the trees ahead. They were safe enough on open ground, but the forest required extra caution. Raider broke the ten-gauge and dropped in two brass shells.

"You probably won't need that," Thomas said. "We came back here at night. No one knows I'm still in the territory."

"I hope not," Raider said.

The scent of the forest was rich and green. Dew still sparkled in the shaded areas of the junipers' soft needles. Mist was also visible in the higher elevations as a cloud rolled in from the west, over the mountains. Raider tried not to indulge his imagination, but it felt damned strange to have the sun behind him and the clouds in front. A gentle rain was starting to fall over the trees.

"Rainin' and shinin' at the same time," Raider said. "Know what that means, Doc?"

"No, but I'm sure you do."

"It means the Devil is beatin' his wife," Raider replied.

"How droll," Doc said dryly.

At first there didn't seem to be a break in the tree line. They stayed outside the trees, riding upward into the rain. Raider felt the double triggers of the shotgun. Where the hell was Thomas leading them?

"You know where you're goin'?" Raider asked.

"Trust me," Thomas replied. "The nearest settlement is miles from here. No one has reason to believe that I have come back here. I was most obvious in staging my departure."

"How long before we go into the trees?" Raider asked.

"We're not," Thomas replied.

The landscape took a quick turn downward, into a slough that had been enclosed by the forest. A stream ran through a rocky bed that ended in a deep pool hidden from the view of the flatland below. The streambed was extremely shallow, and a path allowed Thomas to guide the chestnut mare down through the trees into the water.

"I can't bring my wagon in there," Doc said.

"Leave it," Thomas called back. "Follow the streambed until you see our camp."

"But . . ."

Thomas was gone up the streambed, seeming to disappear into the trees. Doc grumbled as he forced Judith to back the Studebaker into the brush. Raider stayed behind to help cut juniper branches to cover up the wagon. Finally Doc jumped onto Judith's back and urged her down the narrow path toward the streambed. Raider followed on the bay gelding.

"Guess ole Thomas wanted to see his family," Raider said.

"Yes, I suppose so," Doc replied.

The streambed stayed flat instead of sloping up into the trees. As the horse's hooves splashed in the cold mountain water, Raider gazed up at the walls of stone that began to rise on both sides of the stream. It was a narrow fit through a craggy fissure that opened at the end and spread out into a natural chasm.

"Incredible," Doc said. "A dried riverbed with what's left of a runoff stream."

The air was musty and damp. Lichens clung to the walls that rose up about fifty feet. Raider had seen ravines like this one before. They could be really dangerous in the wet season. Especially during the mixtures of spring rain and melting snow.

"Beautiful," Doc said. "It winds around that way. Thomas said to follow the stream."

"Yeah," Raider agreed. "I guess so."

"What's wrong with you?" Doc asked.

Raider pointed toward a tree that had fallen over the wide bed of rocks and boulders.

"Know how that tree got there?" Raider asked.

Doc thought about it. Raider saw the sudden recognition as Doc figured out the geological ramifications of the evidence. Overhead, a rumbling ball of thunder sounded over the mountain. The drizzle was still falling, but heavier precipitation was coming.

"You ever see a flash flood, Doc?" Raider asked.

"No, but I can't imagine that it's pleasant."

"You take a ravine like this, a little heavy rain, maybe some snowbanks up top—boom. A wave runs down the slope faster than anything you ever seen in your life. Takes along anything in its path. A crease like this is just where it goes."

"Well," Doc said, urging Judith forward. "Perhaps we can talk Mr. Thomas and his family into relocating."

They followed the streambed around a bend in the ravine. Camped on a rocky extrusion was Thomas's family. Two black women were tugging at Thomas's arms, trying desperately to tell him something. Another woman—white and well-dressed—stood a few feet away, watching the family gathering. Doc remembered that Thomas had mentioned his brother, but there wasn't another male in the camp.

"Them women's upset," Raider said.

"Yes, we seemed to have arrived at a crucial moment."

They dismounted and joined Thomas. Raider saw that one of the women was younger than the other. Doc tried to listen to both stories at once, but finally had to let the older woman speak first. Thomas introduced her as his sister-in-law, Beatrice.

"I brought these men back to help us," Thomas said.

"My name is Weatherbee," Doc rejoined. "Suppose you tell me what's the matter."

"My man done run off," Beatrice cried.

"Your brother?" Doc asked Thomas.

"Yes, Calvin," Thomas replied.

"When did he leave?"

"Rode out last night," Beatrice replied. "Ain't come back

all night. I know they done killed him."

She was in her thirties, which surprised Doc. He had imagined Thomas's brother to be much younger, as well as his wife. She was a round-hipped, buxom woman, with a broad nose and proud lips. A red bandanna was tied around her head, and she wore an old flour-bag dress.

Thomas's sister was younger and lighter in complexion. She had the body of a girl, with big doe eyes and a narrow nose. Thomas called her Lucy, and she in turn called him Tello. With the silent white woman and Shadow also in the group, Doc found it suddenly confusing, as did Raider, to be in the company of four women.

"My man's gone," Beatrice said. "They gonna lynch him. They gonna come in white robes and string him up."

"Now, now," Doc replied. "Where did he say he was going?"

"Huntin'," Lucy said, her voice as sweet as sugar. "Said he was tired of waitin' for you to come back. Said he was tired of eatin' mush. Said he was gonna shoot us somethin'."

"Then it is logical to assume that he will return," Doc said, turning his attention to the white woman.

At once he ascertained that she was a lady. Immaculately dressed, with a ruffled collar on her blouse, buttoned shoes, and a fine twist to her hair. She had seen the far side of thirty and bore the complexion of someone used to being outdoors. In Boston she would be called a handsome woman and be mistaken for a young widow.

"Your name, please?" Doc asked.

"Margaret Andrews," she replied in a formal tone. "And who are you, sir?"

"Doc Weatherbee, Pinkerton National Detective Agency. This is my associate, Raider. We have come to help Mr. Thomas regain his land. If you would—"

"I want my man, Tello," Beatrice cried.

"Quiet," Thomas replied. "Lucy, take her back to the cave."

The younger girl led a weeping Beatrice back to a recess in the wall of the ravine. A small fire burned inside, and Doc could see that Thomas's family had been calling the place home. He turned his eyes to Margaret Anderson.

"How have you come to be involved in this?" he asked.

"I discovered these people quite by accident," she replied. "I am very sympathetic to their plight, however. I have been offering my assistance for the past three days."

"Did you encourage Calvin Thomas to leave camp?" Doc asked.

"Of course not," she replied. "Why would you have such suspicions about me?"

"Seems kinda funny," Raider piped in. "A fancy woman like you roamin' around out here. What you doin' here anyways?"

"I could ask the same thing of you," she replied.

"Mrs. Anderson," Doc said.

"*Miss* Anderson, thank you. And I will not have you treating me with disrespect. I've been trying to help—"

"She doesn't match the description of the woman in Dodge City," Doc said. "She's slimmer, and her hair is too light."

"How dare you make such personal remarks about me!"

"Did you ride out here?" Raider asked.

"Yes," she replied. "I have a mare tied up back there in the forest. I walked down here to the camp."

"And what business do you have in this region?" Doc asked.

She put her balled fists on her hips.

"Sir! My name is Margaret Anderson, and I will not have you speak to me in this manner!"

"She won't have a lot of things," Raider said. "Now listen up, Miss Anderson. These people have been swindled out of some good sum of money. Me and Doc here are gonna see that they get a fair shake out of it. So anything we ask you is gonna help them—that is, if you can tell us what we might want to know."

"I'm sorry," she said, "It's just that my presence here is of a delicate nature as well. I'll explain if you'll please—"

"Wait," Raider said in a low voice that always froze Doc in his tracks. "Hush up a minute."

"I beg your pardon," Miss Anderson said.

"Thomas, what was that?" Raider asked.

They all listened.

"Thunder," Miss Anderson said finally.

"I don't think so." Thomas gazed toward the entrance to

the chasm. "I don't think that's thunder."

"The thunder's that way," Raider pointed up toward the peak of the mountain. "That's comin' from the trees."

"Gunshots?" Doc asked.

"I don't hear as good as a Injun, but look at Shadow, she can hear it too," Raider said.

The girl was peering toward the juniper tree tops, her forehead wrinkled with puzzlement. She moved closer to Thomas and took hold of his arm. Raider unholstered his .44 and put a sixth round in the empty chamber where the hammer had rested. Doc was slipping a cartridge into his .38 Diamondback.

"Take my scattergun and get the women back into that cave," Raider said to Thomas. "Doc and I are gonna take a look."

"What's going on?" Miss Anderson asked.

"Follow Mr. Thomas," Doc said softly. "Don't worry. I can guarantee your safety."

"I'm gonna need that Henry rifle," Raider called to Thomas.

"Take the chestnut," Thomas said. "She's fast."

"Doc, you ride my bay."

They splashed through the streambed to the fallen tree. Raider reined the mare and turned back to Doc, who had to stop the bay. Raider tossed him the .44 which Doc managed to catch on the way down.

"What the devil are you doing?" Doc asked.

"Take the .44 and use my .30-.30, too," Raider replied. "I'm gonna ride out alone. You guard the pass here."

"I don't think you should—"

"This is better, Doc," Raider said. "I'll keep low. If I can't shoot it with this Henry rifle, I can't shoot it with nothin'."

"I'm coming after you if you aren't back in an hour."

Another volley of echoing gunfire rolled over the trees into the chasm.

"You do that, Doc," Raider said. "You do that."

Raider rode out of the narrow ravine, emerging on the streambed near the forest. The shots were regular, with the sounds of a high-caliber rifle and a smaller gun, maybe a pistol. Raider spurred the mare up the incline into the trees. The forest floor leveled off and then sloped back downward. The mare started slipping on the incline, so Raider tied her up and proceeded on foot.

When he arrived at the edge of the tree line, Raider started along in the shadows. The rain had stopped, but the clouds had smothered up the sun, leaving the sky dark. Suddenly he smelled the sulphur stench of burnt gunpowder. Then voices came through the trees—two of them. Raider dived into the brush, keeping low to ground, listening as a pair of men searched the forest.

"Blood here," said a distant voice. "I got 'im."

"The body there?" said another.

"Nope, but lotsa blood."

"You think he's that darkie we tried to run off?"

"Maybe. Maybe just a straggler. Never woulda seen 'im if we wasn't huntin'."

"The big boss'll be happy if we bring back a dead one."

"We ain't tellin' him about it. Come on, that nigger's dead."

Raider couldn't see them, but he listened to the distinctions in their voices. One was high and the other booming. The deep voice was in charge. Raider listened as they clomped through the forest. One walked softer than the other. A big man and a small man.

Raider heard their horses galloping away over the basin. He rose up out of the brush and started for the direction of the deep voice. The man had found blood. He had talked about shooting a Negro man. And he had believed that the wounded man was dead.

"Thomas," Raider called into the trees. "Calvin Thomas. Your brother sent me to find you. Where the hell are you?"

Raider slipped between the branches, moving slowly through the brush, calling for the wounded man. He heard a sucking noise that seemed to come from a juniper tree. Raider stepped carefully in the same direction. His heart almost stopped when the body fell out of the tree, landing next to Raider's boots. A lanky black man lay on the floor of the forest. Blood covered his entire right side, but after a moment, Raider saw that he was still breathing.

• • •

"He was damned smart climbin' up a tree like that," Raider said. "Musta taken his last ounce of strength. I can tell you he scared me half to death."

Calvin Thomas was spread out on a blanket in the cave. Raider stood over him, holding a lantern for Doc, who was bending to examine the wound. Calvin, who looked to be about thirty, had taken a small-caliber slug in the arm. The wound had bled quite a bit, but he was not in danger of bleeding to death, Doc thought.

"The slug came close to the shoulder socket," Doc said. "If it had been bigger, he might have lost the arm."

"Are you going to take out the bullet?" asked Miss Anderson.

"If I can," Doc replied. "It's a good thing you remembered my medical bag, Raider."

"I didn't have time to cover up the wagon," Raider replied.

"It doesn't matter," Doc replied. "You got him here in time. I think I can keep him from dying."

A muffled scream resounded in the cave. Beatrice lay bound and gagged on the other side of the enclosure. She had been so grief-stricken that Raider had been forced to subdue her and use physical restraint, as Doc called it. Lucy, who kept glancing Raider's way, sat next to her sister-in-law, rubbing her head with a damp cloth. Shadow was also with them, sitting silent and cross-legged.

"Miss Anderson," Doc said. "Will you make sure the other women are all right?"

"Yes, Mr. Weatherbee, I will."

She moved away from the unconscious figure of Calvin Thomas.

"I'm glad he's passed out," Thomas said. "At least he won't feel it when you take out the slug."

Doc poured a tincture all over the wound. When the bullet hole was cleaned, it appeared tiny and harmless. Doc slipped a thin metal instrument into the hole, probing for the piece of lead that had done the damage to the upper arm.

"All of that blood come out of there?" Raider asked.

"Yes," Doc said. "There! I can feel it."

He slid a second probe into the wound and then pressed them together, trapping the lead between the two instruments. Slowly he extracted the slug from the hole. A gushing of blood came out behind the bullet. Doc washed the arm with alcohol and then placed a dressing over the wound.

"He's running a fever," Doc said. "We have to give him water and keep his head cool."

"Will he live?" Thomas asked.

"God willing," Doc replied.

"I've walked away from worse," Raider rejoined. "I think he's gonna make it."

Shadow had gotten up and moved next to Thomas. Her tiny hand was clasped in his big paw. She stared at the body for a moment and then moved away from Thomas to sit next to the fire. Her hands jerked back and forth over the cave floor, scraping up the rich dirt. When she had a pile of earth, she began to make shapes on the cave floor.

"What's she doin'?" Raider asked.

"Sand painting," Thomas said. "Magic for the Navajo. She's doing medicine for my brother."

"Perhaps she's a witch," Doc said.

"That's preposterous," replied Miss Anderson. "If anything has saved him, it's been your doctoring. We can only wait to see what happens to him."

Doc turned toward the woman. It struck him precisely how unlikely it was to find such a lady in the wilds of New Mexico. But then, there had been a lot of things that didn't fit in this particular case. Doc stood up and addressed Miss Anderson with a sweeping bow.

"I'd appreciate the pleasure of your company for an afternoon stroll," Doc said.

"And if I refuse?" she asked.

"Then I shall insist upon your company," Doc replied.

"In that case, Mr. Weatherbee, I shall be happy to walk with you this afternoon."

Doc offered her his arm, and they swept out of the musty cave as if they were on the Commons in Boston.

"He's at it again," Raider said, shaking his head.

"What?" Thomas asked.

"Ole Doc is slicker than a greased-up tadpole," Raider replied. "Don't worry, Thomas. Your brother's gonna make it. He's gonna make it just fine."

"You did a fine job on that young man's arm," said Miss Anderson. "Are you really a doctor?"

"No, I'm not a physician," Doc replied. "I do have a certain knowledge of medical science, however. It helps in my work as a detective."

They were sitting next to a small pool upstream. Doc was looking up at the sky. The rain had moved on, but the clouds remained to make it a chilly, dreary afternoon. He did not seem to notice as much when he looked back into the woman's penetrating brown eyes. There were rings of hazel in her irises.

"I'm from Boston, originally," Doc said. "I attended Harvard and tried my hand as a chemist for a while. I found it rather dull."

He turned to her as if she had to offer the next comment. He was not going to get information out of her by bullying or flattery. She was too strong a woman to respond to force. And it would be a long, unpleasant process to try to break her down.

"You want me to tell you about myself, don't you?" she asked.

"Is there some reason why you can't?"

Her nostrils flared and she threw back her head. "Why must you be concerned with me? Aren't you afraid those men who shot Mr. Thomas will return and try to kill you?"

"No," Doc replied. "Not directly at least. They were chasing him from the south, according to Raider. I don't think they saw us. We came in from the north. They were hunting, and I doubt they were watching for us, anyway."

"Is there nothing you fear?" she asked, one eyebrow raised.

He detected a tempest brewing in her ringed eyes. Her chin was held high, and she looked down her nose at him. He wondered if she was affecting the snobbish attitude or if it came naturally to her.

"Sweetness would be more conducive to the truth," Doc said. "I can be trusted. Raider, too."

"What is it you want to know about me?" she asked.

"Where are you from?"

"Washington. The city, not the territory."

"How on earth did you end up here?"

"My trade," she said. "I've come west to pursue my work."

Doc smiled at her for the first time. She blushed and looked away. The toughness did not suit her as well as the blush.

"I'm an artist," she went on. "And I am also a cartographer, which is the occupation of—"

"Mapmaking."

"Yes. You'd be surprised how many times I have to explain that to people. But now I suppose you're going to say that it's not an occupation for a woman. Or that a woman is strange to have an occupation at all."

"Not at all. I would be more interested in knowing who employs you and how you came to such a prestigious trade."

"Really?" she said, blushing again.

"Only if you want to tell me," Doc replied, careful not to be too forceful.

She was hesitant at first, but when she began to talk, she started to enjoy telling Doc about herself. She had learned the trade of cartography from her father, who had served as an artist and a mapmaker for the United States Department of the Interior. Margaret had preferred learning the trade to the usual domestic path of a young woman. When she was not married by the age of thirty, her father had gotten her a job in his office. The assignment that brought her west was something she had actively sought.

"I'm supposed to sketch and draw maps of the basin area at the foot of these mountains," she told Doc.

"Good Lord," Doc replied. "Do you know why?"

"I'm not sure," she said. "My orders were signed by the Indian Affairs officer in Washington."

"And you have no idea why they want charts of this location?" Doc asked.

"I can only speculate that it has something to do with an Indian reservation in this area," she replied. "That is the first thing that came to mind."

"An Indian reservation," Doc said. "Perhaps you're right.

They are moving the poor souls all over these days. Do you know who might own the land you're mapping?"

"No," she said. "I think they sent me out here just to be rid of me. And I was so happy to go that I didn't ask questions."

Doc smiled again.

"I can't imagine why anyone would want to be rid of you," he said smoothly.

"Why, Mr. Weatherbee. I don't know what to say."

"Say nothing. Let me do the talking, Miss Anderson. Let me tell you what a handsome woman you are. Allow me to commend your bravery and ingenuity. I daresay that most *men* would be afraid to come west for such an undertaking."

"How you talk!"

But he knew she was loving his discourse.

"You've given me much useful information," he said, taking her hand. "And I thank you graciously."

He kissed the back of her hand and might have kissed her lips if Lucy had not come flying around the bend.

"He's awake," she cried. "Calvin is awake. Hurry, Mr. Weatherbee, hurry! He's actin' all crazy-like."

Doc released Miss Anderson's hand and followed Lucy to the cave. Calvin was sitting up, desperately trying to tell his brother something. His voice was low and weak, but he was frantic to get it out. Doc gave him a powder that seemed to calm him down.

"He's delirious," Raider said.

"Did you make out what he was saying?" Doc asked.

"Sheriff," Thomas replied. "He was trying to say that the sheriff was the one who shot him. The sheriff who evicted us."

"This sheriff a big guy with a deep voice?" Raider asked.

"Yes, how did you know?" Thomas replied.

"Let's say I heard him," Raider said. "Let's say your brother's right and work from there."

CHAPTER EIGHT

"It makes sense about the Indian reservation," Raider said.

They were sitting around a fire with Thomas and Miss Anderson. It was late afternoon, with most of the sun already gone behind the mountain. They had sorted it all out and were drawing conclusions on the bank of the stream, away from the cave where the wounded man lay in a fever.

"Somebody's lookin' to sell this basin land to the government," Raider continued. "The same land that went for homesteading ten years back. Buying it back to move Indians here. Somethin', huh?"

"I wonder what they would pay for the land?" Doc said.

"They gave five dollars per acre in Arizona," Thomas replied. "And six in Oklahoma when they moved the Cherokee from North Carolina. I know about Arizona for certain, because I helped move the Indians there. Apaches."

"That's close to half a million at five dollars an acre," Doc said. "A tidy sum."

"Right big hunk of change," Raider agreed.

"I still don't understand about the sheriff," said Miss Anderson, who was perched most ladylike on a stump.

"What don't you understand?" Doc asked.

She had been listening with her pretty chin in her pretty hand, hanging on their every word.

"Why did he try to kill Calvin? And how is he involved with the man who swindled this family?" she asked.

"Obviously the sheriff has to be involved with the man we're calling Wolcott," Doc replied. "Either they are partners or Wolcott simply paid the sheriff to evict the victims."

"Looks like he's workin' for somebody," Raider said. "I heard them talkin' about 'the boss.'"

"At any rate," Doc continued, "the land scam is simple. The front man, Pixton, keeps an eye on the established trails, in this instance the Santa Fe Trail particularly. He looks for people who don't quite understand the way of the territory. Also people who won't necessarily stand a good chance in a trial."

"People of color," Thomas replied.

"In your instance, yes," Doc said.

"But if there are more victims, then why don't they band together and seek justice?" Miss Anderson asked.

"I'll let Mr. Thomas answer that by asking him one question," Doc replied. "What did you think when the sheriff moved you off your new land, sir?"

"I was enraged but not surprised," Thomas rejoined. "The white man giveth, the white man taketh away."

"Precisely," Doc said. "A downtrodden man, a man who is used to injustice, does not fight as strongly as a man who's used to following process of the law. A black man, an Oriental, even a European might not understand their right to a fair trial."

"Or maybe somebody's got a judge in their saddlebag," Raider said. "Keepin' somebody from gettin' a trial. We've seen deals like that before."

"Yes, we can only speculate as to the involvement of the territorial authorities in this matter," Doc said. "For now, we will assume only the facts—and then with scrutiny."

They were quiet for a moment. The afternoon was gone, with only the small fire to alleviate the darkness in the ravine. Thomas had been twisting up a torch out of some twigs. They'd need it when they walked back to the cave.

"Just one thing been eatin' at me, Doc," Raider said.

"I'm listening."

"Well, if this boy Wolcott is gonna sell this land to the gove'ment, then why does he need to be snakin' little people for their life savings?"

"Operating expenses, perhaps," Doc replied. "He has to salt the mine, so to speak, spread out the dust so the mine will look like a bonanza. And you might consider the bribes it would take to make the authorities look the other way. The sheriff has to be paid, no doubt."

"Seems greedy to me," Raider replied. "Might be easy to catch a man with sticky fingers."

"We can also consider the possibility that he doesn't own the land," Doc offered. "He might sell someone else's land just as easily, then deny the whole thing if it ever gets into a territorial court. Given the infrequency of the judge's appearances and the nature of the people bringing the complaint, it boils down to his word against theirs."

"And if he doesn't own it," said Miss Anderson, "then he's selling it to raise capital for something else."

She smiled at Doc. Raider tipped back his Stetson and grinned to himself. He had never seen a lady with so much potential for giving Doc his own medicine. A pretty woman with a bright head was more than a match for the smooth-talking Weatherbee. But then, it would take a lady to put a gentleman in his place.

"Don't much get past this lovely lady," Raider said.

"Assuredly," Doc agreed too dryly.

"I'm overwhelmed that you two are so appreciative of my deductive capabilities," she said.

"Perhaps you'd like to offer your insights," Doc said.

"Well, it seems obvious that you have to go to Santa Fe to find out who owns the land, and to discern the whereabouts of this Wolcott," she replied. "Isn't that right?"

"It makes sense to me," Doc said. "Raider?"

"What about the sheriff?" Raider wondered.

"Do you have something in mind?" Doc asked.

"I could go after him," Raider said. "We could try to get him for shootin' Thomas and the land swindle."

"It could be a path to the top man in the scheme," Doc rejoined. "How would you do it?"

"Well, I got to know where he is."

"Raton," Thomas replied. "About fifty miles north of here. Up near the Colorado border."

"I reckon I could put on a act," Raider said. "I could ride in all mean-like, sayin' that I'm lookin' to work as a corrupt deputy for a dishonest sheriff."

"And assuming that you aren't the only one who has made that request, the sheriff might have another deputy who will blow your fool head off," Doc said.

"You got to have a little more faith in my abilities, Doc. I don't like the notion of splittin' up any more than you do. But you got to do the book work, and I ain't gonna be no help to you in Santa Fe. I can go see the sheriff and meet you later."

"In a pine box, no doubt."

"Don't worry, I ain't gonna get my ass in a sling."

Doc mulled it over. Raider was right. They would save time and effort by branching out. Of course, Doc didn't want to turn Raider loose on the unsuspecting territory. When Doc wasn't around to temper his volatile nature, Raider could leave an awful lot of bodies lying around.

"You can go after the sheriff," Doc said. "But I want you in Santa Fe at the end of the week."

"Sure enough, ole buddy," Raider said with a grin.

"And remember, you're a detective, not a hired gun," Doc warned.

Raider winked at Miss Anderson. "He worries about me more than my momma."

"Yes," Doc rejoined. "The difference being that your mother loves you."

"I'll cut and run if it gets messy," Raider said.

"We'll both leave in the morning," Doc added.

"And me?" Thomas said.

"You'd be too visible," Doc said. "I suggest you stay here with your family. Your sisters will need you now that your brother is hurt."

"I understand," Thomas said.

"This is all very exciting," said Miss Anderson. "You men certainly know what you're doing."

Lucy's voice called to them from the cave, interrupting any further praise from the lady. Dinner was ready. Lucy had been stirring a big pot of pinto beans that she had seasoned with salt and venison. Doc had fashioned a tin of cornbread earlier, and Shadow had contributed a pile of wild scallions.

"Y'all come 'fore it's cold," Lucy called. "You too, Mr. Raider. Hurry now."

Raider hoped Thomas hadn't noticed the way his sister had been looking at Raider. Those lovey-dovey doe eyes were trouble. Not that Lucy wasn't a cute little thing. And she was probably old enough for ... But Raider couldn't bring himself to go after a man's sister, no matter how willing she was. It didn't matter if the man was black or white.

"Shall we go," Doc said, offering Miss Anderson his arm.

"I'm gonna stay here for a while," Raider said. "I'm gonna clean my gun and then I'll come eat directly."

Thomas stuck the torch in the fire and held it to light their path. He called back to Raider, seemingly unaware of his sister's flirtation. He assured Raider that there would be a plate of beans left for him. Then the three of them disappeared up the bank with only the glow of the torch visible in the darkness.

Raider was so hungry that his stomach was growling. The aroma of the beans had reached him on the night air. But he was sure as hell going to stay away from Lucy Thomas. He had seen her brother blow off a man's head at a hundred yards. Mr. Thomas was just too good a shot.

When the fire began to die, Raider walked back up toward the cave. The recess was shallow enough for him to see everyone by the fire inside. Lucy was sitting next to her brother. Beatrice was wiping her husband's forehead, while Shadow moaned in a low incantation. Doc and the lady were curled up like kissing cousins.

"I'll take the first watch, Doc," Raider called from the shadows. "Relieve me at midnight."

"Aren't you going to eat?" Doc called.

"I lost my appetite," Raider replied.

He was lying. He could still smell the beans, and the aroma of coffee was in the cool air. Lucy was staring into the night, trying to see him. She was trouble, if it had ever been born.

From his saddlebags Raider took some dried venison and a box of sulphur matches. He gathered twigs in the dark and piled them in a dry spot between three rocks. Shielding the sulphur match with his hands, he ignited the twigs, feeding them kindling until the bright fingers of flame were big enough to accept a small log. He leaned back on a patch of sand and watched the fire creeping over the log.

The clouds had disappeared to the east, leaving the night

sky as clear as a cold-water spring. No moon, but stars were bright enough to see by once your eyes got used to it. Still mountain air with the noise of the stream to lull you into sleep. He was nodding when the footsteps came up from the cave. It had to be one of their party.

"Doc?" Raider said.

No reply. He smelled the beans again, stronger than ever. A whiff of perfume in the air. The footsteps came closer.

"You don't like my cookin'?" said Lucy's honeyed voiced.

Raider jumped to his feet.

"What are you doin' comin' out here?" Raider asked.

"My brother said I oughta bring you a plate of beans," she replied, stepping gingerly into the ring of the firelight. "He said he could hear your stomach growlin' all the way down here."

"Aw, he can't do it," Raider replied.

"You don't like my cookin'?" she repeated.

"Gimme that plate," he replied.

She thrust it toward him. The tin plate was covered with pinto beans and chunks of venison. A hunk of cornbread rested in the center, along with several raw scallions. Raider could not remember when anything smelled better to him. He forgot about the girl, slurping the entire meal with a wooden spoon.

"You shore was hongry," Lucy replied. "I ain't never seen a man eat so fast."

"You better git on back up to that cave, girlie," Raider said.

"I ain't doin' it till I want to," Lucy replied.

Raider swallowed the last piece of cornbread. He stepped down to the stream and drank from his cupped hands. Lucy dogged his steps, taking the plate and washing it in the stream. When Raider started back up to his fire, Lucy was still beside him.

"Look here, Lucy," he said. "You got to go back in there with your brother. You can't hang around with me."

"What if I want to? Nobody can stop me," she replied.

"Your brother can sure as hell stop *me*," Raider said. "He knows how to stop people. Believe me, I've seen him."

"He ain't sayin' nothin'," Lucy said. "Besides, I ain't no little girl no more."

"How old are you, anyway?" Raider asked skeptically.

"Nineteen," she replied.

"More like fourteen," Raider said.

"No, I ain't. You ask my brother, he tell you," she insisted.

Raider shook his head. He told her that he didn't care if she was a hundred and nineteen, she couldn't stay with him while he stood watch, and that was final. Until she began to cry.

"Aw, come on," Raider said. "That ain't fair. Damnation, Lucy, why do you want to stay here with me anyway?"

"Ever'body up there got a man but me," she replied. "Tello with his squaw, them two fancy folk together, and Beatrice got my brother. Ever'body sittin' with somebody, but I ain't got nobody to sit with."

"Aw, hell," Raider said. "You can sit with me. Just don't do nothin' that's gonna make your brother shoot me."

Raider sat down again by the fire. Lucy sat next to him, but not too close at first. The flames seemed to put Raider in a trance. He did not notice as she inched toward him. Or at least that was what he let her think for a while.

"What are you up to, girl?" he said, startling her.

"I wanna put my head on your shoulder," she replied.

She started bawling again, sobbing so loudly that Raider was afraid her brother might hear.

"All right," he said. "You can put your head on my shoulder, but that's all."

Lucy rested her soft face on Raider's shoulder. Her bushy hair brushed against his cheek. She smelled of something damned good and downright intoxicating. Raider pushed her away from him for a moment.

"What's that smell?" he asked.

"The fancy woman give me some soap," she replied. "I washed in the stream with it. Do you like it?"

"Nineteen, huh?" Raider said.

"What?"

"Yeah, I like it," Raider said.

"Can I put my head on your shoulder again?"

"Yeah, you can do that."

She lowered her head again. Raider slipped his arm around

her shoulder. He thought it wouldn't hurt to curl up with her. She was sweet and soft. Thomas wouldn't kill him if he just found them keeping warm by the fire. As long as it didn't get any further along.

"You a nice man," Lucy said, purring like a mountain lion.

Her hand started over his chest, running through the hair inside his shirt. Raider caught her wrist and pushed it away. She persisted, trying to undo his buttons.

"Whoa, lady," Raider said. "Don't start nothin' you can't finish. What the hell would your brother say?"

The damned fire seemed to be getting hotter.

"What you think he's doin' with that squaw?" Lucy asked. "He's slippin' it to her ever chance he get."

"Lucy, don't talk about your brother that way."

"He my brother, but he a man, too," she cried.

"Shh, they'll hear. How the hell do you know about these things?"

"I told you I'se nineteen. I just look young cause I worked in the house. You look older when you're sharecroppin' like Beatrice and Calvin."

"Maybe you ought to go back up there with them."

"I wanna put my head on your shoulder," she insisted.

That damned fire. She went back to work on him. He tried to resist one more time. Lucy practically shouted at him that he was not her first man, not even her second or third. And if he didn't watch out, she was going to tell her brother and really make trouble. Her head fell once again, and her hand started down the line of his belly.

"Don't fight me, boy," she teased. "The only time I'm trouble is when I don't git what I want."

Raider reclined on the sandy bank, where granules of fine silt had gathered, forming a cushion over the rocks. The fire crackled until finally it began to die. By that time, Lucy had unbuttoned his pants. Her hands were rubbing his crotch, first through the worn denim and then inside. Raider's cock was swelling so much that she had trouble getting it out.

"Damn it," she said. "God was as good to you as he was to the colored men I knowed."

"Well, you got it, woman," Raider said. "Now what you gonna do with it?"

She replied by stroking his stiff phallus with her hands. Raider didn't miss the fire. He was sweating underneath his shirt. Lucy shifted until she was kneeling over him, still jerking his cock. Her thighs spread, and she guided Raider's hand to her wet crotch. She was not wearing any underwear.

"Rub it all around," she said, hunching his fingertips.

Raider ran his fingers over the folds of her vulva. The wetness flowed onto his hand. He had seen some steamy women, but Lucy, he thought, had sprung a leak. Her body shook and quivered as he obeyed her request.

"Put one inside me," she groaned, still at work with her skillful hands.

Raider slipped a finger into her tight vagina. He wondered if she would be able to take him. It wouldn't matter if her brother came down the streambed with his Henry rifle in hand.

"I wanna have it," she said. "Do it to me, white boy."

She hiked up her dress, falling back on the sand, spreading her brown thighs. Raider reached up, rubbing his hands over her small breasts. She grabbed his wrists and pulled him down on top of her. Her hand wrapped around his cock, and she guided him into position. Raider forced his hips down, evoking a grunt from Lucy's lips.

"Slower," she groaned. "Ooh, that feels good."

Her cunt expanded to accept his rigid length. His hips started up and down. She responded with an upward motion of her buttocks, bouncing off the soft bed of sand. Raider felt awkward with her, even though he was inside. He half expected to hear the report of Thomas's .44-40.

"What's ailin' you?" Lucy said, looking up at him.

"Nothin'," he replied.

He started to take it slower, feeling himself inside her, concentrating on the way her muscles gripped him. Her perfume made him forget everything. For a minute, he was back with Claire, in her soft bed, doing all those things she had made him do.

Their bodies began to rise and fall in one motion. Lucy had

wrapped her arms and legs around him, holding on as he drove his thick cock in and out of her. Suddenly he didn't care who heard them. He wanted to come inside her and have his pleasure. If Thomas wanted to take a shot, he would have to kill them both.

"Oh, now you're tellin' the truth," Lucy moaned.

His cock bulged with the fiery discharge. The girl's body shook with spasms of its own. They were both sweating. It was several minutes before the night chill got through to them. Raider pulled out with a sloppy noise.

"I got to build a fire," he said.

"Go ahead," she replied. "But you're goin' to teach me again. I ain't never had it from a man like you."

"I thought you said I wasn't your first," Raider said.

"You ain't first, but you the best," she replied.

Raider pulled up his pants and built another fire. He looked back toward the dark cave to make sure Thomas wasn't coming after him. Topping a man's sister shouldn't have been so enjoyable. But then, who had topped who? The girl was next to him again in the dim light.

"Ain't you goin' back to the cave?" Raider asked.

"We got till midnight," she replied. "I heard the doctor man say that."

"Lucy, I don't think it's right for us..."

Her hands were at work again, trying to make him hard. She was like a cowboy with a new gun—just had to be playing with it all the time. Raider leaned back again, thinking that he shouldn't be screwing on his watch, but unable to stop the woman who attended his groin. She didn't take it in her mouth like Claire, but her fingers were enough to revive him.

So he put it inside her again, using his hips until she extracted a second burst. But even at that, she refused to leave him alone. She was forcing her nipple between his lips when they heard the footsteps on the rocks.

"Git on outta here," Raider said. "It must be midnight already."

He pulled up his pants as she bolted into the darkness. She obviously ran past the man who was coming toward Raider. He tossed a small bundle of twigs to spark the remaining coals.

As the flames illumined the area, he saw Thomas coming down the bank. Raider decided not to deny anything. He would just fess up and then let Thomas kill him. He wouldn't even offer a fight.

"Did you get your beans?" Thomas asked.

"I swear I didn't wanna do it."

"Eat beans?" Thomas asked.

"What?"

"You didn't want to eat your beans?" Thomas asked again.

He had seen his sister run by him, away from the fire. They had been down by the stream for almost five hours. What the hell did Thomas think they were doing?

"Lucy's a good cook," Thomas said, ignoring Raider.

"Yeah," Raider replied. "I ate them all."

"She can be a bit . . . rambunctious, at times," Thomas said. "I have very little control over her when she gets her head up."

"Rambunctious, huh?" Raider said. "You said it, not me."

Thomas laughed. "Go get some sleep, Raider. Doc will be down to relieve me at four."

Raider got up and started back to the cave. His legs were wobbly. Surely Thomas had known what his sister was up to. And he didn't seem to care. Like he knew Raider didn't have a choice. Some people were just damned hard to figure.

He climbed into his bedroll. Beatrice was still awake, tending her husband. Doc and the lady were asleep on opposite sides of the fire's glowing coals. And Lucy had wrapped herself in a blanket, sitting next to Shadow who still worked at her sand painting. Raider rolled over and closed his eyes. It was a moment before he heard Lucy's giggling. He managed to go to sleep in spite of it.

The next morning, as Raider ate his fry bread, he tried to avoid looking into Thomas's eyes. He was sure everybody had figured out what had happened between him and Lucy, although nobody seemed to pay much attention to him, including the girl. Instead they hovered over the sleeping, peaceful figure of Calvin Thomas, whose fever had broken during the night.

"He's going to make it," Doc said. "You were right, Raider."

"We better get ridin'," Raider replied.

"What's wrong with you?" Doc asked.

"I'm just itchin' to get movin'. There's been too much lollygaggin' on this job. I think it's about time we started workin'."

"I couldn't agree more," Doc said.

"I'm goin' to saddle up," Raider said. "I'll meet you at the wagon. I got to get me a disguise."

"Yes, I'll be right behind you."

Doc watched as Raider quickly hitched up his saddle and then hurried down the stream. He had never seen his partner so eager to start work. Miss Anderson came up next to him and took his arm.

"Where's your friend going?" she asked.

"To my wagon," Doc replied. "I'll join him momentarily. I want to check on young Thomas before I go. One more look to make sure there are no complications."

"You did an extraordinary job in treating him," she said. "You should have been a real doctor."

Doc peered into her adoring eyes. He would have kissed her right there if the others had not been close by. They were calling him to look at the bullet wound. Their kiss would have to wait.

Miss Anderson sat behind Doc as Judith's sure hooves took them through the rocky fissure at the entrance to the ravine. Her arms were wrapped tightly around his waist, and her ample breasts pressed against his back. Her scent was maddening enough, but to have her so close was extreme torture. As Doc urged Judith up the incline into the trees, his senses were full of the lady from Washington.

"My horse is tied close by," she said. "I left the feedbag on the poor thing."

"Then I wouldn't worry," Doc replied.

They came out of the trees and started for the wagon. When Doc looked down between the trunks, he saw that the Studebaker was uncovered. The bay gelding was tied behind the wagon, but Raider was nowhere in sight. The air was deceptively still and quiet.

"What is it?" asked Miss Anderson.

"I don't know," Doc replied. "Something isn't right."

"Hold your hands in the air," said a raspy voice. "Don't make no sudden moves. I might have to drop you."

A tall, bald-headed man stepped out of the trees. He had a pistol trained on Doc. A gash, the result of a recent wound, showed on the man's scalp. Doc felt Miss Anderson trembling behind him. She had her hands over her head.

"No need for alarm," Doc said. "You may put your hands down."

"But he has a gun!"

Doc threw one leg over Judith's back and hopped down to the ground. He strode confidently over to the bald man and pulled down the bandanna that covered the man's face.

"An excellent disguise, Raider," Doc said. "Why on earth did you shave your head?"

"How'd you know it was me?" Raider said.

"The gun," Doc replied. "Of course, that's a minor thing. I know you well enough to recognize your sidearm. Better let me take a look at that gash on your head."

"Better watch out for that lady," Raider said.

Miss Anderson was coming toward them with an angry face.

"How dare you frighten me like that?" she cried. "Is that your idea of a joke?"

"I just wanted to see if I could fool anybody," Raider said. "Looks like I fooled you, Miss Anderson."

"Ooooh, I am going to find my horse, Mr. Weatherbee," she cried. "You might consider yourself fortunate to see me again."

She stormed off into the trees.

"If you're lucky, maybe a Injun will git her," Raider said.

Doc was not amused. He turned back to Raider and started to say something. But then he reasoned that it would be easier to let the entire matter be forgotten.

"Why did you feel possessed to shave your head?" he asked Raider.

"I want to look mean when I go into Raton," he replied.

"You certainly look different," Doc said. "Mean or not, I couldn't say."

"I put my Stetson away in the wagon," Raider said. "I'm taking this felt hat."

In the floppy hat, with a week's growth of beard and the scar on his bald head, Raider would not have been recognized by Allan Pinkerton himself. He had also taken a ratty undershirt and a leather vest from Doc's trunk of disguises. With a hunting knife in his boot, he appeared to have wandered in off some godforsaken badlands plain. He led the bay gelding from behind the wagon and jumped into the saddle.

"Adios," he called to Doc. "See you in Santa Fe at the end of the week. Don't let her run you ragged."

He spurred the gelding and bolted over the basin. As Doc was hitching up Judith to the wagon, Miss Anderson reappeared with a pair of horses walking behind her. She cast a pouting glance at Doc and then turned away, starting down the line of trees. When Judith was in harness, Doc went after her, figuring that he could spend at least the rest of the morning trying to get his kiss.

CHAPTER NINE

Raton was one of those jerkwater towns that grew up around a trading post at the foothills of the southern Rockies. It was a stage stop, and rumor had it that the railroad would be there one day. But until then it was going to stay small: Population ninety-one, declared the plank sign at the edge of town. A dirty hole in the wall, but the kind of place where men found the privacy to carry on unlawful enterprises. Raider thought it would look good to any man who felt as wet and cold as he did. He wanted to be warm and dry after the fifty-mile ride.

The drizzle had started about an hour before Raider saw the town in the distance. Another cloud was rolling over the mountains. Raider slowed the gelding as he rode onto the main street. He was deliberate in his trek up the muddy avenue. He wanted everyone to notice him. He even threw off his hat so everyone could see the skinhead with the scar on his noggin. The powers-to-be in Raton would immediately get word of the stranger in town—the baldy with a mean look in his eye, the tall ape in the gray slicker.

Raton had a saloon for the peaceful citizens and a jail for the ones who weren't so meek. Raider rode past both, keeping his eyes straight ahead, gambling that he wouldn't be bushwhacked—right away. They'd feel him out if he played it right, just to see if he could be of some use to them. He wondered if it would be the sheriff who called him out.

The Muddy Dollar Saloon was across the street from the livery; good placement, Raider thought. He stabled the gelding and splashed across the street into the dismal tavern. Bare walls, a makeshift bar, crude wooden tables. The bartender was a nervous man with a skinny mustache. Two wrinkled barflies shared one of the tables. Otherwise the place was empty.

Raider let the swinging doors close behind him. He stood for a moment, allowing them to take a look at him. Then he strode confidently to the bar, slapping a silver dollar on the rough-cut wood. The bartender's nervous eyes flashed back and forth between the dollar and Raider.

"It ain't got mud on it," Raider said. "You got any whiskey that ain't homemade?"

"Rye," the bartender said. "Come in from Kansas on the stage."

"Will that buck buy a bottle?" Raider asked.

"Buy two," the bartender replied.

"Give 'em to me," Raider said. "You got anything to eat?"

"Pot of stew in the back."

"Don't tell me what kind of stew," Raider replied. "Just bring me a bowl."

He threw another dollar on the bar and grabbed the two bottles. As the bartender went to fetch the stew, Raider found a table close to the barflies, who had been studying him. Nothing incited talk like a stranger in town. Excitement, maybe even somebody getting killed.

Raider poured himself a drink of the rye. It wasn't bad, but it burned a little going down. As he served himself a second glass, he noticed that one of the barflies kept staring at him. He was an old man who looked like he had crawled out of the mountains. Raider leaned back and glared at him.

"What you lookin' at, old-timer?" Raider asked.

"Nothin', sir, nothin'," the old man called back.

"Get over here," Raider barked.

The old man was suddenly trembling. Raider had scared him half to death. The other man was shaky too.

"You old-timers want this bottle?" Raider asked.

That got their attention. They were still scared, but scared like the coyote waiting for the mountain lion to leave the kill. Raider pushed the bottle of brown liquid toward them.

"Come over and tip one," Raider said. "Come on, I ain't gonna bite you, boys. Wet your whistles."

Slowly they got up and ambled over to Raider's table. He poured them a drink and watched them as they gulped it down. Doc would have called them rummies. Old-timers who'd do just about anything for a drink. A pitiful sight, Raider thought. He had suddenly lost his taste for the rye. The rummies looked back at him with hopeful eyes. Raider started to pour and then drew back as they extended their glasses.

"Not yet," he said. "You boys is gonna have to earn it. You do what I tell you and you'll get both bottles."

"Both," said one of the rummies. "He's gonna give us both."

"What we have to do?" asked the other, who seemed skeptical.

"Run tell the sheriff that Ram Tatum is sittin' in the Muddy Dollar wantin' to see him," Raider replied. "Tell him there ain't gonna be no trouble as long as he talks to me."

They talked it over between them for a minute.

"That's all?" said the skeptical man.

"Run tell him and come back here to get your bottle."

"You said two bottles!"

"You ain't gonna git nothin' if you don't vamoose," Raider said. "Now what'll it be?"

Both of them hurried off as fast as they could, shuffling out of the swinging doors into the misty rain. The bartender brought Raider a steaming bowl of meat stew. It didn't taste like beef, but it was hot. Raider spooned it down, keeping an eye on the door. He finished his dinner before the two rummies came back.

"You tell him?" Raider asked.

"He's told," said the skeptical one.

"Take that whiskey and get out of here," Raider said. "I don't want nobody around when I do my business."

He didn't have to tell them twice. After they were gone, Raider fixed his chair so he was facing the door with his back to the wall. He propped up his left leg against a wall stud and put the sawed-off scattergun on his thigh. Then he covered the ten-gauge with a fold from his slicker. His hand was underneath the damp coat with both fingers wrapped around the shotgun's dual triggers. The .44 was riding his hip. He threw back the other fold of his slicker so he'd have an easy drop with his gun hand. He was ready for them. All he could do was wait.

* * *

Miss Anderson had a second horse to pack all of her equipment and belongings. Doc marveled that she was able to get so many boxes onto one horse's back. All day she had been unpacking different cartons, producing sketch pads and pastel chalks and finally a box camera that sat on a tripod like a bulky spider body. She had taken great pride in setting up her photographs.

"I don't suppose you know much about photography," she said to Doc.

"Well, let me see," Doc had replied. "I believe silver nitrate is the basis for the process, isn't it? Yes, I thought so. Daguerre developed the plate negative, but I believe a chap named Talbot has invented a type of negative paper. As far as artistry, I admire the work of Matthew Brady, who studied—"

"The Civil War."

"Yes. Now, is there anything else that you would like to suppose about me?"

"I have work to do, Mr. Weatherbee."

"I shall be happy to assist you, Miss Anderson."

So Doc had helped her for the morning and for the better part of the afternoon, until the thunder clouds came and chased them into a small box canyon to the south. Miss Anderson had discovered the place two days before. A ledge of stone jutted out about ten feet above the canyon floor, providing a dry space for them and their animals. The rain had soaked them thoroughly.

"You'll be delayed in your ride to Santa Fe," she said.

"I was hoping you might be heading that way," Doc replied.

She was drying her hair with a thick towel. She stopped and smiled at Doc. He put his hand behind her head and leaned down to kiss her. She enjoyed it as long as she dared and then broke away. Doc would have been disappointed if she hadn't broken away. A lady always exercised restraint.

"I may be riding into Santa Fe," she said. "My work here is done. I still have to write my calculations."

"I have delayed too long as it is," Doc said. "Although the company has been well worth it. Would you be offended if I told you that it is extremely rare and precious to find such beauty and intelligence in one woman?"

"I don't think I would be offended at all, Mr. Weatherbee," she replied.

Doc laughed. "I can't believe you camped out here all by yourself."

"I am not helpless," she replied.

"And I respect you greatly for that. And for helping the Thomas family."

"I have always been driven to help those more unfortunate than myself," she said simply.

"As soon as the weather breaks, we'll ride for Santa Fe," Doc offered.

"I find that agreeable."

Doc slid his arm around her shoulder and pulled her close to him. Their bodies fought the chill as they huddled together. It was a feeling Doc wished he could know more often. Marriage was impossible for a man who stayed on the path of some wrongdoer. But a woman like Margaret Anderson made a man have peculiar thoughts about settling down.

"I think it's letting up," she said.

He kissed her cheek. She pressed herself against him for a moment and then rose to her feet. Doc got up and started to put Judith back into harness. He gazed out over the canyon, wondering if the mud would hold his wagon wheels. The rain hadn't lasted long, so it wasn't too soggy.

"We'll have to stay on the high ground for a while," Doc called to Miss Anderson. "But I think that—"

"Mr. Weatherbee," she said in a petrified voice. "Please help me. Come here and bring your gun."

Doc grabbed his .38 Diamondback, thinking she had discovered a rattlesnake that had been flushed from its hole by the rain.

"What is it, Margaret?" he said.

She was hiding behind her packhorse, gazing out into the canyon. Her eyes were straining in the afternoon shadows. Doc peered out too, trying to discern what had captured her attention.

"Wolves," she said. "Two of them. I saw them stalking us. They moved behind those rocks there."

"I don't think that's likely," Doc replied. "Wolves usually

travel in packs, and even if they did come into this canyon, our scent would drive them away. They're afraid of humans."

"There!" she said.

Doc's eyes detected the movement between two boulders. He watched the area, staring at everything and seeing nothing in the same instant. Something was getting closer to them. He wrapped his finger around the Diamondback's trigger.

"Move your horses toward my wagon," Doc said.

"But—"

"Just do it!"

As Miss Anderson moved behind him, the two animals came out into the open. They weren't wolves, but rather big black dogs—German shepherds. Doc had seen such dogs before back east. White teeth were bared, and a low growling hung in their throats.

"Slow," Doc said to Miss Anderson.

"Where did they come from?"

"Get on the wagon."

Doc was backing away from the dogs, keeping the Diamondback pointed toward their muzzles. When one dog started forward, Doc burst off a round that hit the dirt in front of the animal. Instead of scaring it off, the shot provoked both dogs into attacking at lightning speed. Doc dropped to one knee, taking aim, hoping that he could kill them before they covered the fifty yards between them. . . .

The rain stopped but the clouds stayed, bringing an early dusk to Raton. Raider had been waiting for almost two hours, drinking cups of hot coffee, watching the swinging doors. A small crowd had gathered on the wooden sidewalk outside the Muddy Dollar, anticipating the promise of trouble from the big man inside. Raider tensed when he heard uneven footsteps on the wooden sidewalk. The crowd parted and a small man pushed through the swinging doors.

"You Tatum?" the man asked in a high voice that Raider recognized from the forest.

"Maybe I'm Tatum," Raider replied. "Who the hell are you?"

In the dim lamplight of the saloon, Raider couldn't see the

man's face. His hands were held out away from his hips. He wasn't going to pull on Raider. He was the scout, the one who had been sent till the sheriff decided what he wanted to do about the tall stranger. As he came closer, Raider got a look at his ratty, pointed face.

"I ain't packin' a hog leg," the man said.

"Yeah? That ain't what I heard," Raider replied, freezing the man in his tracks. "I heard you was awful big shootin' people with that twenty-two squirrel gun of yours."

The man squinted at Raider.

"How you know I got a twenty-two?" the man asked.

Raider had gambled about the squirrel gun. Doc had taken a twenty-two slug out of Calvin Thomas's arm. The rat-faced man had put it there. A little rifle for the little man. Lucky guess.

"I know a hell of a lot of things," Raider replied.

"Aw, you don't know nothin'."

"You tellin' me you didn't shoot a colored man about a day's ride south of here?" Raider challenged.

"How'd you—"

"He got it in the heart," Raider lied. "You shoot pretty good with that squirrel gun."

"Who the hell are you?" the man cried.

"I'm a spook," Raider replied. "I'm the Devil, mister, and I'm gonna send you straight to hell if you don't get out of here, pronto. I ain't talkin' to nobody but the sheriff. You run on back and tell him what I said."

The little man started backing slowly toward the swinging doors, keeping his hand out to the side. Armed or not, he wasn't going to pull on Raider. He didn't have the guts.

"Maybe sheriff don't want to come," the man said. "Maybe he's gonna send his deputy. Maybe his deputy is more than you can hold, Tatum. What do you say to that?"

"Get gone, boy!"

The little man flew through the swinging doors and down the sidewalk. Raider checked his weapons again. The next man through the door wouldn't be a messenger. Raider stood up and leaned against the wall. He pulled one arm out of his slicker and let the sleeve hang loose. Under the slicker, he held the shotgun in his left hand. Then he took off his hat and tossed it on the table. Another pair of feet hit the sidewalk boards, clomping slowly toward the swinging doors. A dark shape appeared in the threshold.

"Tatum?" said a steady voice.

"I'm in here," Raider replied.

"How you want it? Face to face?"

"If you're man enough," Raider replied. "Show yourself. I'll wait for you to draw."

The doors swung open. Raider couldn't believe what he saw. Johnny Denton came into the saloon. Even in the dim light, he could tell it was him. He was toe to toe with the Oklahoma Kid. Fate could sure deal some funny cards.

"They say you're a spook," the Kid said. "They say you know things about people."

"That's right," Raider replied.

"What do you know about me?" the Kid asked.

"Johnny Denton," Raider replied. "You like to play poker, don't you, boy? The Oklahoma Kid likes to play poker."

Raider thought he saw a nervous smile on the Kid's face. He hadn't been afraid of Raider until then. The Kid's gun hand came down to his side. Raider watched his fingers instead of his face. It was obvious that the kid didn't remember Raider. The skinhead threw him off.

"Lot of people know me," the Kid replied.

"I know you tried to rob a train in Kansas about a week back," Raider replied. "I know you ran off with some Pinkerton's poker money. You're waitin' for your gang too. Only they ain't gonna be here."

"Is that right?" the Kid smirked.

"Billy Simpson is dead," Raider replied. "So are the other three boys. I know that for a fact."

"Who the hell are you, mister?" the Kid said.

"Ram Tatum, I told you. Either we do business or I'm gonna have to go right straight to the sheriff."

"You have to go through me," the Kid replied.

"That's a mighty short walk. Seems to me the big train robber is sinkin' low by workin' for a jerkwater sheriff in a mud town like this. What's your momma gonna think of you, Johnny boy?"

The Kid's hand moved. Raider raised the scattergun and let both barrels fly. A buckshot fist removed most of the Kid's midsection. He fell to the barroom floor, his pistol halfway out of the holster. As the smoke settled, the first brave citizen stuck his head through the door.

"Tell the sheriff Ram Tatum's lookin' to talk to him," Raider barked.

The citizen disappeared down the sidewalk. Raider strode over to the corpse and looked down. His stomach turned at the sight of Johnny Denton's steaming guts. The bartender came out of the back to survey the carnage.

"Is that the end of it?" the bartender asked.

"Get over here," Raider said.

The bartender obeyed him without questions.

"Go through his pockets," Raider said.

"What?"

"Do it, see if he has my . . . any gold on him," Raider replied.

As the bartender went through Johnny Denton's pockets, Raider reloaded the scattergun. His hands were a little shaky. They were always shaky after he killed someone. He couldn't just blast someone and not feel something about it. At the bar, he poured himself a shot of rye and gulped it down. Then he put the scattergun on the bar and turned toward the door.

"He don't have nothing," the bartender said.

"Keep searchin'."

The crowd outside announced the sheriff's arrival. Heavy clomping on the boards. A big man pushed his way through the citizens into the saloon. He wasn't taller than Raider, but he had about a hundred pounds on him in weight. A lot of it was blubber, but that didn't make Raider feel any more confident. He had seen a lot of fat men who were quicker than they looked. The voice was the other man from the forest.

"What the hell you doin'?" the sheriff said to the bartender.

"Tatum made me go through the Kid's pockets, Mr. Bridge."

"You had business with the Kid, Tatum?" the sheriff asked.

"Yeah, he took somethin' of mine," Raider replied. "And

I sure as hell didn't expect to run into him here."

The sheriff pushed back his hat, relieving some of the shadows that hid his sagging face. He had a red, whiskey complexion and a face like a bloodhound. Raider watched his gun hand as it came up and scratched his bulbous nose.

"He ain't got nothin' on him," the sheriff replied. "Rode in here busted, lookin' to hire on. Said he had men comin' after him, but they ain't showed."

"They won't," Raider replied.

"You took 'em?"

"In spades, Mr. Bridge. Is that what they call you?"

"Just Bridge," the sheriff replied.

He kicked the body of the Oklahoma Kid.

"He's dead all right. Some of you boys get in here and get the body over to Doc Tavish. Move, I said!"

Several frightened citizens came in slowly, keeping one wary eye on Raider as they picked up the corpse.

"Kinda glad you did that," Bridge said to Raider. "I wasn't lookin' forward to his boys showin' up either. I like to keep a tight noose on things around here."

"You shoulda faced him down yourself," Raider replied.

"Probably would have, if you hadn't showed. Since you did, I figured I'd let you two boys slug it out. Now, they tell me you been wantin' to talk."

"Looks like you're gonna need a new deputy," Raider replied. "And since I killed your old one, I reckon I'd like to apply for the job. Less'n you think I should challenge you for your job."

The sheriff laughed and shook his head.

"No need in shootin' a perfectly good deputy," he replied. "I'll pay you day wages. There'll be the reward on the Kid too. You can have half."

"Do I get a badge?"

Bridge only laughed and told him he could sleep over the bar where the Kid had been staying upstairs. Mr. Bridge liked to compromise, Raider thought. He wasn't the kind of man who would face you down, which meant that he was the kind of man who'd keep an eye on you. The kind of man who'd shoot you in the back when he wanted you out of the way.

• • •

Before Doc fired another shot, a man's voice called out, reverberating through the box canyon, stopping the two dogs in their tracks. Doc kept the Diamondback trained on them, waiting for the man to show himself. The animals continued to growl, flashing their teeth to remind Doc that they were ready to attack at the next command.

"Call them to you," Doc cried to the unseen voice. "Do you hear me? We're clearing out. Call them off."

Doc couldn't look away long enough to catch sight of anyone. He didn't want to give the dogs any advantage. They were only twenty or so yards away from him. He thought about shooting them anyway, but decided it would be useless if their owner had a rifle.

"What are you doing on my property?" said the man's voice.

"Answer him, Margaret," Doc said.

"I'm from the Department of the Interior," she replied. "I've come to chart and map this area. My associate—"

"That's enough," Doc said. Then to the hidden man: "Show yourself. There's no need for hostilities."

"Drop the weapon," came the reply.

"Call the dogs off first!"

After a moment, the man whistled and the dogs ran back toward the mouth of the canyon. Doc lowered the weapon and hurried back to the wagon. Miss Anderson was sitting on the seat, gazing out toward the direction of the voice.

"Why did you stop me?" she asked.

"I was afraid you were going to betray me as a Pinkerton," Doc replied.

"Wouldn't that have been the proper way to identify yourself?" she challenged.

"Not to an unknown party," Doc replied. "As agents of the law, we are frequently maligned by the criminal type. And, if this man turns out to be—"

"Come out of the canyon," the voice said again. "I assure you, you won't be harmed."

"What shall we do?" asked Miss Anderson.

"Exactly what he said to do," Doc replied.

Doc tied Miss Anderson's horses to the back of the wagon and then jumped into the driver's seat. He put his pistol between him and the lady, evoking a delicate shudder from her. Doc touched her hand and looked into her frightened eyes. "Danger is not nearly as exciting as one thinks," he said. "Don't be afraid. I don't believe this gentleman is going to do us harm."

"How can you be so sure."

"Shh, we have to move forward or he'll become suspicious."

Doc urged Judith toward the mouth of the canyon. The ground was muddy, but it was holding the wagon wheels well enough. As they came out of the canyon, they saw the gentleman in his fancy clothes. He was much more dapper than Doc and appeared quite regal with the two burly dogs flanking him right and left.

"You must excuse my boys," the man said in a slick voice. "They've only been with me for a week or so. When they seem disturbed, I give them their head and let them go. Sorry if they scared you. I had no idea that the government had sent anyone as yet. Please accept my apologies. I'm Simon Wolcott."

Doc could not hide his smile. The adrenaline had started flowing when he challenged the dogs. Now he was looking down at the one man who had seemed the most elusive.

"My name is Weatherbee," Doc said. "This is Miss Margaret Anderson. We've been sent to chart this property. Is it yours?"

Simon Wolcott smiled and laughed. He did not answer Doc, but instead affected an air of cordiality that was hard to challenge. Walking up to the wagon, he extended his hand for a weak handshake.

"Are you camping nearby?" he asked.

"We had considered going into Santa Fe," Doc replied. "Perhaps you could suggest a suitable hotel."

"Are you through with your calculations?" Wolcott asked.

His face was thin, with slitted eyes. A pencil-thin mustache had been meticulously cultivated over his narrow mouth. The smooth hands had never done a day of manual labor. Foppish, Doc thought.

"We have most of our readings," Miss Anderson replied. "I need an office to draw the—"

"Then you shall stay at my hacienda," Wolcott replied. "I would have it no other way."

"That won't be necessary," Doc replied.

"I insist," Wolcott replied, as full of syrup as a hotcake. "After all, we are bent toward the same task, aren't we?"

He laughed again. His voice gave Miss Anderson a creepy feeling. Doc touched her arm to put her more at ease.

"Perhaps we should accept the gentleman's invitation," Doc replied. "Separate rooms, of course."

"Well," she said. "If it's no imposition."

"Nonsense," Wolcott replied. "Allow me to finish my business at hand and we shall ride for my hacienda."

"Thank you," Doc replied, tipping his derby.

Wolcott started toward his palomino mare which was tied nearby. He pulled himself into the English saddle and cantered over the plain with the dogs behind him. A squire, Doc thought, riding to the hunt with his hounds.

"I don't like him," said Miss Anderson.

"Nor do I," Doc replied. "But he's the man we've been searching for, the man who swindled my client."

"Wolcott! Of course!" she exclaimed. "What did he mean by that remark, we're both working for the same goal?"

"Obviously he expects to benefit from giving us room and board. He believes he has the advantage with the Interior Department. Perhaps he will tell us exactly what he expects to gain."

"I still don't like him."

"Would you prefer to go to Santa Fe?" Doc asked.

"No, no, I want to be with you."

"It may get hazardous ahead," Doc said.

She nuzzled her face into his arm. Doc touched her hair and looked in the direction that Wolcott had ridden. His figure was still barely visible on the southern ridge of the basin. Doc extended his telescope and saw the dapper gentleman standing with a group of Chinese men and women. A family perhaps. Wolcott was standing next to them, gesturing out toward the basin.

"What's he doing?" asked Miss Anderson.

"Selling a piece of land," Doc replied.

"Again?"

"Apparently Thomas was not the only fly to fall into the spider's trap," Doc replied.

He was grinning. The game had begun again. Only this time, Doc was going to be one of the players. And Raider? How would he find Doc if Doc was not in Santa Fe? They should never have split up. Doc had known it all along. But it was too late. Doc would have to take his chances alone, hoping Raider would catch up somewhere down the road.

CHAPTER TEN

"Raton's a pretty dead town," Bridge told Raider. "They tell me the railroad's comin', but I can't see it."

A bottle of red-eye whiskey sat on the table between them. When the mess was cleaned up, Bridge offered to buy Raider a drink. As the new deputy, Raider could hardly refuse. He listened to the fat man talk, wondering if such a harmless-looking old hound could be involved with the people who cheated Thomas. Bridge wasn't the kind of man who liked head-on confrontations. Maybe he just got what he wanted by cheating. Maybe he didn't care who was on his side, just as long as his ally was quick with a gun.

"You sayin' there ain't much doin' for a man in this town?" Raider asked.

"Oh, there's geetus to be made," Bridge replied, refilling his glass. "Just have to go to Santa Fe to spend it."

"How much money am I gonna make?" Raider asked.

"Five dollars a day," Bridge replied. "That ain't bad for a deputy's wage. Course, you'll be on night duty. The Kid had to take it too. Ain't much to it. Rattle a few doors at ten and then at six in the morning. I'll relieve you at eight. You can sleep days over the Muddy Dollar. It's quiet then."

Raider nodded. "Just one thing," Raider said. "I been hearin' that some real money's comin' into this part of the territory. Are you in on that?"

"Maybe," Bridge replied, eyeing Raider with caution. "Who told you there was?"

"The Kid said he was onto somethin'," Raider replied. "Guess he's sorry to miss out now."

"He ain't sorry about nothin'," Bridge said.

"You tellin' me there ain't no big money?" Raider asked.

Bridge snorted and wiped his nose with his sleeve. He pushed his chair back a little, which prompted Raider to slide his hand around the sawed-off. Bridge shook his head.

"Ain't no need for that," he replied. "I ain't fool enough to take you on. I just ain't takin' kindly to a bunch of strangers comin' in here and wantin' to cut in on my business."

"Look, Bridge," Raider said. "I ain't got no beef with you. You sent the Kid and I killed him. So I had personal business with him and woulda killed him anyway. You said you really didn't want him around. Well, I'm thinkin' that you don't want me around maybe."

"I didn't say that."

"Well, I'm thinkin' it," Raider replied. "I'm also thinkin' that you either need a deputy or you don't. I'm askin' if you're hirin', but I ain't gonna try to muscle my way in and then catch a bullet later. I'll work for you, but only if you need me."

Bridge tossed down a swallow of red-eye and slammed the glass on the table. Raider poured his glass full again.

Bridge laughed. "I like you, Tatum" he said. "You don't cig around with a bunch of bullshit."

"I'll stay or go, peaceable both ways," Raider replied.

"You can stay, boy," Bridge said.

He leaned forward and crooked his finger at Raider, meaning for him to lean in too, so they could talk privately.

"Don't worry about the big money," Bridge said. "A quick man like you can get his hands on plenty. You ain't afraid of using a little friendly persuasion, are you?"

"Ask Johnny Denton," Raider replied.

Bridge laughed again. "Come on, I'll show you the jailhouse."

They left the Muddy Dollar and crossed the dark street. The jail was a one-hole, stone hovel that couldn't hold a pickpocket, Raider thought. Bridge matched a hurricane lamp and pointed toward the key on the wall.

"That's how you lock 'em up," Bridge said. "Anybody goes rowdy, just haul 'em in. Check doors like I said. Hell, don't take but ten minutes. Sleep if you want to."

"Ain't much to it, is there?" Raider asked.

"No, but stick with it, Tatum. You and me can rack up if

we play our hands close to the table. If you need me, I got a room back of the general store. Don't wake me up less'n it's life and death. Pocket watch in the desk if you need to know the time."

Raider watched him go, settling in behind the small desk. He put his feet up and listened to the night sounds. As Bridge had said, the streets were dead quiet. After an hour or so, he got up and gazed out of the smoky window. The only illumination on the streets was the glow from the Muddy Dollar. Those lights disappeared an hour later.

At ten o'clock, Raider walked the dark streets just in case the sheriff was watching. Bridge was cautious, and he was definitely waiting for something big. But whatever it was, it sure as hell didn't appear to be in Raton. Doc was always telling him to look for things that weren't obvious. Raider couldn't see a damned thing on the dark streets. A lot of times, it seemed like Doc didn't know what the hell he was talking about.

Simon Wolcott's hacienda had been built by an early Spanish nobleman who had ventured bravely into the wild New Mexico Territory. High walls, originally protection from Indians, rose around the stucco house, giving it the appearance of a citadel rising out of nowhere on the range. According to Wolcott, they were ten miles east of Santa Fe. As the three of them rode through the wooden gate into the walled fortress, Doc was thinking of ways to get away from the hacienda without attracting too much attention. He needed to check a few things in Santa Fe.

"A marvelous villa," Doc said.

"Thank you," replied the mannered Mr. Wolcott. "I enjoy the Spanish architecture."

"It is lovely," said Miss Anderson.

Three buildings had been erected on the quarter acre that the walls enclosed. When Doc asked, Wolcott explained that the large stucco building was the main house, the stone structure was the kitchen, and the wooden barn served as the stable and the servants quarters. A small garden had been planted next to the kitchen. If evening had not been upon them, Doc would have been able to examine the buildings more carefully. He marked the locations and tried to estimate the distance between them.

Wolcott dismounted and clapped his hands. "I hope we did not miss dinner," he said.

A young Mexican boy came up to take Wolcott's horse.

"Let Julio tend to your animals," Wolcott said.

"What about your dogs?" Doc asked.

The two German shepherds were never far from their master's feet. They seemed calmer, but Doc didn't trust them. He had seen their teeth.

"They stay by the door," Wolcott replied. "Now I will show you to your quarters and you may freshen up before dinner. My wife and I will be happy to have such civilized guests for dinner."

Doc relinquished the reins to the Mexican boy. With Miss Anderson on his arm, he followed Wolcott into the main house. The halls were cool and narrow, winding back into a series of larger rooms. Miss Anderson was given a neat room with a table. Doc had the room across the corridor. Wolcott informed them that a servant would call when dinner was ready.

"I'll have them cook something even if we're late," Wolcott replied.

"Perhaps then we can discuss business," Doc replied.

Wolcott laughed again and then left them. Doc waited for a while and then slipped across the hall to Miss Anderson's room. When he came in, he caught her half dressed.

"Mr. Weatherbee!" she cried, pulling a sheet to her bosom.

"Please," Doc said. "You must forgive me. I had to speak to you before we went to dinner."

"You shouldn't have—"

"Yes, I know," he replied. "But you must do me one favor. When we go in to dinner, take the lead in the conversation. Describe what you've been doing. Try to get Wolcott to talk about his business. But don't make it too obvious."

"Can't you do that?" she asked.

"Wolcott's smart," Doc replied. "Look how quickly he manuevered us into his territory. I don't want him to think I'm prying. He might get suspicious."

"All right," she replied. "But you must give me back my privacy, sir."

"Yes, of course. Oh, one other thing."

"What?"

"You have the loveliest white shoulders I've ever seen."

She didn't thank him, but her shoulders quickly turned a bright red color.

"Leave me," she cried. "Before I scream."

Doc slipped out, smiling deviously. The hunt was on, all of the participants pulled on by the intrigue. But the smile disappeared when he realized how alone he was in Wolcott's house. Raider might have been a nuisance, but he was a good man to have around if you needed a backup.

Simon Wolcott's dining room was illuminated by six flaming torches that protruded from the wall. Below the torches rested an oak table that appeared to Doc's calculating eye to be about eight feet long. The table had been dressed with a fine linen cloth and then set with expensive china and silver. Doc had sipped his California port wine from a crystal goblet that a Mexican servant refilled from a larger, silver decanter. At the beginning of the meal, Doc had tried to make dinner converstion with his host. However, he had been rudely interrupted by Mrs. Simon Wolcott, who sat across from him. Lorna, as her husband called her, had been drinking heavily of the same port. She had been paying too much attention to Doc and was on the verge of creating a scene.

"Drink, Mr. Weatherbee," she said in a sultry voice. "It makes me feel good. Maybe it will have the same effect on you."

Doc only smiled and tried not to look at her, a task at which most men would have failed. Her hair and eyes were dark brown; Spanish descent, Doc thought. The nose had a slight, endearing crook that gave her face character. She had thick, full lips and a proud chin. When she leaned forward, her dress revealed the deep canyon of her bosom. As the Dodge City printer had said, she was the kind of woman that you might remember a long time after you saw her.

"Would you have more wine, *Miss* Anderson?" Lorna asked.

"I think I will excuse myself," Miss Anderson replied.

"Weren't you going to say something about your work?" Doc said to his lovely associate.

"She's drunk," Miss Anderson whispered to Doc. "And she's practically fawning all over you. I won't stand for it."

"She has a slight headache," Doc said as Miss Anderson left the table.

"Oh, then it's just the three of us," Lorna declared. "Shall we have brandy on the verandy? Ha, ha, I made a joke."

Doc smiled graciously, casting a glance toward his silent host. Simon Wolcott seemed preoccupied. He had not given a second thought to his wife's flirtation with Doc. Wolcott sat at the end of the table, content to keep to himself. There was really no way to bait him without appearing too obvious.

"Simon, are we going to have brandy on the verandy?" asked Mrs. Wolcott. "Mr. Weatherbee and me...and *you*, Simon. Would you like that Simon, the three of us together..."

"Shut up, Lorna," Wolcott replied in a cold, reptilian voice. Then, in a more friendly tone. "Mr. Weatherbee, allow me to apologize for my wife. Sometimes she drinks a little more than she should."

"I drink a lot more than I should," Lorna replied. "And you should too, Simon. It might make a man out of you."

"I said shut up," Wolcott replied.

"To hell with you," she cried. "I'm going to get my brandy. On the verandy. Ha, ha."

She was tipsy as she got up. One of the servants tried to take her arm but she broke away, declaring that she could walk by herself. For an awkward half minute, she staggered through the dining room. When she had made her exit, her husband let out an exasperated sigh.

"I'm terribly sorry," he said.

"Sir, believe me," Doc replied, "in no way do I wish to encourage any sort of flirtation with Mrs. Wolcott. If you'd prefer that I take my leave..."

"Nonsense," Wolcott replied with an unnatural calmness. "You're to have complete run of the place. The servants are yours to command. Pay no attention to the...to my wife."

"Thank you," Doc replied. "I certainly hope you get a chance to look at our work on the charting of your property."

"My property," he said ambivalently. "Yes, I shall be happy to take a look."

"Tomorrow then?" Doc asked.

"No, I must leave in the morning," he replied. "In fact, I shall probably be gone when you awake. I'll be away until tomorrow night, so perhaps the day after tomorrow."

"Be careful when you're traveling about," Doc said. "This area is notorious for Indians and highwaymen. Of course, if you need someone to ride with you..."

"Not necessary," Wolcott replied. "I'm taking my surrey. The boys—my dogs, that is—will ride with me. And I have a certain knowledge of firearms."

"Well, some parts of the territory are rougher than others," Doc said. "Are you going far?"

Wolcott leaned back in his chair and studied Doc with his slitted eyes. A man who trusted no one. A man who clearly did not love his beautiful wife. He ran a palm over his slick hair.

"You seem to know a lot about the West for a man who comes from Washington," Wolcott said.

"Too many adventure books," Doc said quickly. "I presume too much. Are you from this area, Mr. Wolcott?"

"Good night, Mr. Weatherbee."

"Yes, well, I appreciate your hospitality, sir, and I thank you from the..."

But Wolcott had already moved out of the torchlight. He had dismissed Doc the way a boy king dismisses his schoolmaster. He was certainly not going to volunteer any information. Doc would just have to poke around himself.

"Mr. Weatherbee."

The errant Mrs. Wolcott was coming down the hall, her brandy in hand. She spilled a drop on her bosom as she staggered. Doc rose from the table and went in the opposite direction. He had to assuage Miss Anderson's delicate sensibilities. She was pouting in her room.

"What are you doing here?" she cried.

"Margaret, what has gotten into you?" Doc said.

"I saw the way she looked at you," she replied. "You liked it. You smiled back at her."

"I didn't smile at her, I smiled to be polite. I didn't want to upset her husband. Although he didn't seem to care. He certainly wasn't ready to talk."

"Something about him makes me...afraid. And her...how could you flirt with a woman like that?"

"I wasn't flirting with her," Doc replied. "And a lot of help *you* were. You refused to talk as much as Wolcott."

"Shh, listen."

Footsteps resounded in the hallway. Clumsy feet, the steps of a woman who had drunk too much. She staggered to Doc's door and knocked lightly. Her slurred voice called sweetly for Doc. When she didn't get an answer, she slammed her fist on the door.

"Damn it all," she muttered.

They waited for her to move out of the hall.

"She was coming for you!" Miss Anderson accused.

"It doesn't matter," Doc replied. "I'm leaving here in the morning."

"Leaving?" she said, suddenly frightened. "I'm going to be alone with him? And *her?*"

"Listen to me," Doc said. "Wolcott is leaving too. You continue to work on your charts."

"But where are you going?" she asked.

"Santa Fe. If anyone asks, tell them I had to send a wire to Washington. I'll be back tomorrow evening."

"Doc, don't go," she pleaded.

"I have to. I have to check on the property rights to that basin land. And I should send a report to the home office. Of course, you're welcome to come with me. I can understand your not wanting to put yourself in a precarious position."

"Do you want me to stay?" she asked, her face turned up to his.

"You might learn something useful if you remain here, but I leave it totally up to you."

"I'll stay," she said meekly. "I want to help you. I...I think I've fallen in love with you, Doc."

He gazed into her adoring face.

"Margaret, I assure you that I would never intentionally have anything to do with a woman like Lorna Wolcott," he said.

"Kiss me," she replied. "Kiss me and hold me."

Doc pressed his lips to her mouth, wrapping her in his arms. He would stay with her until dawn, when he heard Wolcott pulling out. Then he would wait a half hour and set out for Santa Fe.

CHAPTER ELEVEN

Raider had dozed through the night, waking at intervals to look at the pocket watch. At six A.M. he opened his eyes and shook his groggy head. Sunlight had appeared on the smoky glass window of the jailhouse. Raider took his feet off the desk and grabbed the sawed-off shotgun to take with him on his morning rounds.

Raton wasn't much. Besides the saloon, the jailhouse, and the livery, there was only a peckerwood general store and a rooming house. A few citizens had small homesteads farther down on the plain; Raider had seen them when he rode in. Mostly the place was damned quiet and too spooky. Morning fog was receding through the forest slope above the town, silently winding around the trunks of juniper trees. Raider started across the street to the general store.

Winslow Sundries had been freshly painted on a sign over the general store's front porch. Somebody had just bought them a business, Raider thought. He wondered if the "W" and "S" had any connection to the earlier pattern that Doc had established. Raider didn't have too much faith in that handwriting stuff. It seemed like a real lame way to identify someone.

He started down the alley between the store and the rooming house. At the rear of the store, he gazed through a tiny window to see Bridge sleeping on a narrow cot. The sheriff snored like a hog, Raider thought. As Raider turned away from the window, he caught sight of a small shed behind the general store. Doc always said to check out everything. He walked back through high weeds to the bare-planked structure.

There weren't any windows, only a sign on the door warning everyone to "Stay out of here or the sheriff will git yu." A steel lock secured the heavy door. Raider stepped back, trying to find an opening in the planked roof. Nothing. He glanced back at the door. The hinges were on the outside.

"Well, now," he said to himself. "That wasn't so smart."

He used the butt of the .44 to tap the bolts from the centers of the three brass hinges. They were fairly new, so the bolts came out without too much trouble. When the door fell open, Raider eased it out to allow himself enough space to slip into the shed without disturbing the lock.

It was dark inside, but even with the little light that spilled in, Raider could tell what was stacked against the walls. Cases of ammunition, all .44-.40 cartridges, were lined up in rows five feet high, forming a second wall around an object that had been covered with a white cloth.

Raider stepped forward to strip the cloth away. Resting on a small cart was the pride of Mr. Gatling himself. Repeating death. You could chop down a redwood tree if you had enough ammunition. And Bridge seemed to have plenty. Where the hell had he gotten a Gatling gun and who was he going to use it on? Raider threw the cloth over the wagon and slid back out of the shed.

He lifted the heavy door and fitted the hinges together. Then he put the bolts back into position and tapped them down. As he turned back toward the store, holding his .44 like a hammer, the sheriff came around the corner. Raider flipped the .44 in his hand and thumbed back the hammer.

"Hey, Tatum, watch out, it's me fer Chrissake," Bridge cried.

"I don't like nobody sneakin' up on me," Raider replied.

"What the hell are you doin' back here anyway?" Bridge said. "I didn't tell you to come out here."

"You tell me to check the town, I check everything," Raider replied. "Besides, I thought I heard somebody back here. And them hinges was loose on your shed back there. I tapped them down."

Bridge gazed out toward the shed. The ground behind it dropped slightly and then rose back into the woods. He glared at Raider.

"You see anybody?" Bridge asked.

"No," Raider replied.

"You look in that shed?"

"No, it wasn't open," Raider replied. "I told you, the hinges was just loose."

Bridge rubbed his chin. "That doesn't mean nothin', Tatum. Maybe you just heard a deer. They get this close sometimes."

"Yeah, I reckon," Raider replied.

"And don't come back here no more," Bridge said.

"I won't."

"Good. Now, let's git goin'," Bridge replied.

"Where?" Raider said. "I ain't had much sleep."

"You said you wanted some big money," Bridge replied. "I'm gonna take you to meet the boss. He likes to know who's workin' for him. Besides, we got business, and I need you to ride along. Make sure you bring that scattergun."

The *boss*, Raider thought. That was getting somewhere. Doc hadn't wanted to split up, but Raider knew it was going to work. He followed Bridge through the alley, reminding himself not to let the sheriff get behind him.

Doc was hopeful as he rode into Santa Fe. The town at the end of the Santa Fe Trail had been around since the first Spanish settlers, serving as a nucleus for the southwestern territory. As a seat of government, any records concerning land grants and homesteading would be kept at the territorial courthouse. Doc stabled Judith and then started down the main street.

Santa Fe was busy. East of town, near the stockyards, a herd of cattle had started to move out. Storekeepers were in their windows, beginning the business day by turning around their CLOSED signs to OPEN. Doc wondered how many more people the railroad would bring. As the last stop on the trail, Santa Fe had spread out considerably. It was even starting to smell like a city.

The courthouse wasn't open yet so Doc walked to the telegraph office. He wired the home office about his location, reporting only that they were still gathering evidence. He asked for any pertinent information on Simon Wolcott and all of his aliases. He didn't wait for a reply, but told the telegraph operator that he would return later.

The courthouse was open when he went back. A young,

white-faced clerk sat behind a desk laboring over a large black ledger. He glanced up at Doc through his wire spectacles. Doc presented his Pinkerton credentials and informed the young man that he was pursuing an investigation.

"What have you come for?" the young man asked.

"You don't seem surprised," Doc replied.

"These records are the best in the territory," the young man replied bluntly. "What have you come for?"

Doc showed him the piece of land on a map. The young man could not find the purchase records simply from the location; he needed a name. Doc gave him Wolcott's and then the aliases when Wolcott's name revealed nothing. The aliases were futile efforts as well.

"Do you have a record of homestead properties?" Doc asked.

"Yes," he replied. "But you'll have to look through it yourself. There are more than a hundred names. I have other work to do."

"Hurry then," Doc replied. "You'll save time for both of us."

Doc spent the better part of an hour examining the original certificates of deed for the homesteaders. They weren't in any particular order. Toward the bottom of the pile a name jumped out at him—Pixton. Doc read the coordinates on the deed. It was the same location that Thomas had given him before. Liam Pixton had homesteaded the basin in 1841. The same man who had helped to swindle Thomas.

Lorna Wolcott's maiden name was Pixton, so it was not hard to figure out why Wolcott had married her. He certainly hadn't shown much interest in his wife at the dinner table. She was simply part of his scheme. But where was her father? Doc hadn't seen him at the hacienda.

"Have you found something?" the young clerk asked.

"Yes," Doc replied. "Are these grants still the legal titles to the land?"

"No," the clerk replied. "They've been transferred."

"Would you see if you can find this deed?"

The clerk cross-referenced the homestead grant with the latest title. A month before, the land had been transferred into two names—Simon and Lorna Wolcott. Their marriage had taken place a week before the transfer. Liam Pixton's death certificate had been dated two weeks prior to the marriage. All of the documents were in order. The clerk was proud of his efficiency.

"Anything else I can do for you?" he asked.

"Yes," Doc replied. "Can you tell me where I might find the local agent for Indian affairs?"

Franklin Dearborn, the Indian agent, was an irresponsible sort. Doc found him in his office, playing stud poker with four other men. When Doc introduced himself, Dearborn didn't bat an eye. He tossed down a whiskey and dealt the next hand. Apparently he had been playing cards all night.

"What can I do for you, Mr. Pinkerton?" he asked.

"It's a matter of delicacy," Doc replied. "If we might speak in private?"

"Cut loose, mister," Dearborn said. "I can't fold this hand."

He was the embodiment of sloth and inefficiency, Doc thought. Dirty, unshaken, unkempt. He had probably won the job by default and was hanging on, drawing his pay without too much effort.

"I was wondering if you had received any word of a new Indian reservation in this area?" Doc asked.

Dearborn looked away from his cards for the first time.

"Reservation? Hell no. Where'd you hear that?"

"You mean you haven't heard a single mention of a land purchase east of here?" Doc asked. "Land for another reservation?"

"No, I ain't heard squat. I think somebody woulda told me about somethin' that big. Besides, nearest reservation is southwest of here. And believe you me, them Apaches ain't goin' nowhere."

It was possible that someone as inept as Dearborn had simply failed to read his mail or to find a directive at the telegraph office. Or perhaps Miss Anderson's speculations about the reservation had been wrong. But if there wasn't going to be a reservation, then why was she sent to chart the basin land in the first place?

"You look as frazzled as a bear cub trying to hump a greased water bucket," Dearborn said to Doc.

"I intend to report your conduct to your superior," Doc said. "Good day, Mr. Dearborn."

"Sum bitch!"

Doc returned to the telegraph office and asked the operator if there had been any recent messages neglected by the Indian agent. There hadn't been any telegrams for Dearborn, and the Pinkerton home office had not yet sent a reply to Doc's wire. Doc penned a message for Raider, who would check with the telegraph office as a matter of procedure when he hit Santa Fe. Doc described Raider's appearance to the operator and told him to hold any replies from the home office.

As Doc strode back toward the stable, he pondered what he had learned. There wasn't going to be an Indian reservation on the basin land, but Wolcott might still be brewing something big. From the look of his hacienda, he was obviously used to the finer things in life. The land swindle was probably the financing for everything, although Doc could not help but feel that a man as shrewd as Wolcott had greater designs.

Liam Pixton, deceased, had been used and then discarded. Doc wondered how he had died. The death certificate had stated natural causes, but that was a matter open for investigation. Documents could be falsified with the right payoff.

With Judith in harness, Doc started back to Wolcott's hacienda. His slippery host had said he was returning late in the evening. That would give Doc enough time to ask Lorna Wolcott some questions. The investigation would not advance until he had a few direct answers. To break a chain, you found the weakest link. When Doc mulled it over, the obvious weak link was Liam Pixton's beautiful daughter.

Raider ate the dust from Bridge's Appaloosa for half a day as they rode hard to the southwest. At midday they reached a series of holding pens big enough to accommodate a large herd of cattle. The dandy was waiting there for them, sitting back in his surrey with the two wolf dogs flanking him. Raider didn't like him right away, but he tried to hide it. The boss insisted on shaking hands with Raider. He had an awfully weak grip.

"Is he fast with a gun? " the dandy asked Bridge.

"Never seen faster," Bridge replied. "He's pretty good with a scattergun, too."

"Yes, I'll bet he is," the dandy said. "He's a big one."

Raider didn't like the tone of the dandy's voice or the way his slitted eyes glared at him. He didn't like those damned dogs, either. His hand rested on the saddle horn where the sawed-off hung.

"Did you bring the money, Mr. Wolcott?" Bridge asked.

There it was, Raider thought. The connection. Doc would be tickled to hear about it. Raider smiled.

"Something wrong, Tatum?" Wolcott asked.

"Er, no, sir," Raider said. "I was just admiring your dogs."

Raider did not like the way Wolcott smiled back.

"Would you like to come closer and pet them?" Wolcott asked.

"No, sir," Raider replied. I'd sure as hell like to shoot them, he thought.

"Take off your hat," Wolcott said.

Raider removed the floppy felt hat. Wolcott was acting damned strange. Bridge seemed a little nervous too.

"A shaved head," Wolcott said. "My, my, I do believe I like it, Mr. Tatum."

Raider put his hat on. Wolcott's laugh grated on him. He thought he could save everyone a lot of trouble by just shooting Wolcott right there. Of course, that would only put Raider in hot water with everyone. Procedure was a pain in the saddle.

"The herd is moving in from the west," Wolcott said. "You'll be able to hear them soon. Have you ever punched cows, Mr. Tatum? Or may I call you Ram?"

"I've done about everything, Mr. Wolcott," Raider replied.

"I was hoping you had," Wolcott said.

Raider was starting to simmer a little. Wolcott had a sissy-boy way of putting things, he thought. A gentleman didn't have to be weak. Doc had proved that. Bridge sensed Raider's irritation and stepped in to ease the tension.

"If you give me the money now, I can ride south and meet the foreman," Bridge said.

"No need to rush," Wolcott replied. "I can continue my conversation with Mr. Tatum."

But they heard the cattle in the distance, which gave Raider and Bridge an excuse to ride out and help with the herd.

"He's kinda funny-like," Bridge said as Raider rode next to him. "Just try to ignore it."

For the rest of the day, Raider was a true cowboy, helping to move the herd into the holding pens. He counted over three hundred head. When the last steer was in, Bridge found him and told him to follow along. They rode back to the surrey.

Wolcott handed over a large strongbox that Bridge gave to the trail boss of the drive. The trail boss counted the money and then gave Bridge a bill of sale. They shook hands and the trail boss moved out, leaving a few men to guard the herd until Bridge's own men arrived. Bridge and Raider returned to their smiling boss.

"It's all done," Bridge said. "I got the price you asked. Three hundred and twenty head. Shorty's out raising a crew right now."

"It's moving along perfectly," Wolcott said. "You know, the Interior Department sent two representatives to chart the land, a man and a woman. They're staying with me now."

Doc and Miss Anderson, Raider thought. That was just like Doc. Leave it to him to find Wolcott before Raider. He was just plain lucky. At least they were both on the right track. "Someone will be coming to look at the herd fairly soon," Wolcott said. "I'm going to convince them that I can feed every Indian in New Mexico and Arizona. Then you'll become my foreman, Bridge, and we'll have a legitimate income. How about you, Mr. Tatum? Would you like to be rich?"

"As much as any man, I reckon."

"It will be dark soon," Wolcott said. "I don't want to travel alone on the prairie. I want Mr. Tatum to come with me."

"If you say so," Bridge replied. "Any objections, Tatum?"

Raider shook his head. He hated going with Wolcott, but he figured it would mean a reunion with Doc. He wondered what kind of luck Doc was having at his end.

"All right, you ride with him," Bridge replied. "But be back in Raton as soon as you can. Mr. Wolcott, is that other thing set?"

"Yes, Mr. Bridge, you may be on your way."

The sheriff galloped north, leaving Raider to start along next to the surrey. He refused to look at Wolcott. Even so, the damned dandy wouldn't stop talking.

"I think you'll like my hacienda," he said. "It's about four hours from here. Of course, we could stop along the trail if we get tired."

"No we can't," Raider replied.

"What do you mean?" Wolcott asked.

"I mean I can sleep in the saddle," Raider replied, mindful of the two dogs. "So let's just ride in silence."

"Are you always this forceful?" Wolcott asked.

Raider did not reply. He simply rode forward, keeping the dandy and his dogs in the range of his peripheral vision. If Wolcott made a move of any kind, he'd find out about the forcefulness of a ten-gauge load of buckshot.

In the late afternoon, when Doc returned to Wolcott's hacienda, he didn't have to look for Lorna Wolcott. She appeared at the door of his room, clad only in a flimsy peignoir. Purple light filtered through the dusty window, striking her voluptous body through the silky fabric. Doc had just taken off his coat and was sitting on the edge of the bed, preparing to loosen his spats.

"Let me do that for you," Lorna said.

"No, that's quite all right."

But Doc knew that she would probably not talk unless he played her game. He allowed her to kneel in front of him. Her hands worked until his overgaiters were tossed aside. Then she ran her fingers up Doc's legs.

"I saw you ride in," she said. "I wanted to see you last night, but I couldn't find you."

Doc smelled the sweet wine on her breath. Moving hands rested on his thighs. Her large nipples brushed against his knees. The scent of a feminine form was quite compelling, he thought.

"I fear discovery by your husband," Doc said. "This isn't right, you know. Perhaps—"

"Don't worry about Simon," she replied. "He isn't much of a man. Not like you. Why do you think he has those dogs?"

"Isn't he going to return?" Doc asked.

"Yes, but he won't be looking for me. Kiss me, Mr. Weatherbee."

She pressed her lips to Doc's mouth. Her tongue darted between his lips, probing with a desperate hunger. Doc grabbed her shoulders and pushed her away.

"Mrs. Wolcott, we shouldn't be doing this."

"Damn you, are you going to be like my husband too? Am I so repulsive?"

"On the contrary," Doc replied. "You're very appealing."

She smiled when he said that.

"Thank you," she replied. "I'd never know by the way my husband treats me."

"We should talk," Doc said.

She shook her head and rubbed her hands along his thighs.

"I like to talk afterward," she replied. "Unless, of course you don't fancy women."

Doc could not very well refuse the challenging note in her voice. He touched her face, gazing into her dark eyes. She pressed her lips to his again, and this time he returned her affections. As they kissed, Mrs. Wolcott's hands began to work on his clothes. She whisked off his shirt and then pushed him back on the bed. As her fingers loosened the buttons of his trousers, Doc felt the rising erection between his legs.

"You're hard," she said. "Oh, thank you, thank you."

He thought she was a bit too dramatic, but the results were no less pleasurable. Her soft fingers manipulated the expanding shaft as her lips roved over Doc's chest. Doc wondered how Simon Wolcott could resist his vigorous bride.

"Touch my breasts," she whispered.

Doc complied, feeling her healthy bosom with his fingertips. The nipples hardened under his touch. Lorna was moaning, lifting herself onto the bed. She pulled Doc's head to her chest. His tongue replaced his fingertips on her nipples.

"Touch me between the legs," she said.

She certainly knew what she wanted, Doc thought. He slipped his hand down her soft stomach to the wet crevice between her rough thighs. A gasp escaped from her throat. Her ample hips began to grind under his ministrations.

"You know just where to touch me," she moaned.

They continued fondling each other, using eager hands to build the intensity of their feverish gropings. Lorna pushed Doc away, tearing at the folds of her peignoir, stripping the scant garment from her full body. She reclined on the feather mattress, her big breasts spilling to both sides of her chest.

"Get on top of me," she moaned.

"Not just yet," Doc replied.

"But I want you inside me."

"Momentarily," Doc said, "But first . . ."

His hands stroked her thighs. She shivered, biting her finger. Her soft skin was warm to Doc's touch. As he pushed his fingers into her vagina, he lowered his lips to her nipples. If she wanted excitement, he was going to torture her with desire.

"Deeper," she whispered.

Doc worked his finger in and out of her, listening to her heavy breath, watching as her breasts rose and fell. She was entirely at his command. He leaned over and kissed her ear.

"You're very beautiful," he said. "I don't see how any man can resist you."

"Put that thing inside me," she replied, grabbing his stiff cock. "I want it now."

She pulled at Doc's pants, which were resting on his thighs. He managed to get out of his trousers, joining Mrs. Wolcott in her total nakedness. She spread her legs, allowing him to settle into the gap between her thighs.

Doc felt her wetness against the tip of his cock. She didn't even reach down to guide him in. Instead, she arched her back and accepted his full length in one thrust. A glazed look came into her eyes as he filled her. He started to move, but she grabbed his backside, digging her sharp fingernails into his ass.

"No, don't move," she moaned. "I want to feel it in there."

She squirmed underneath him, and the muscles of her vagina tightened around his penis. Her hips started moving again. Doc held on when she started bucking like a wild mustang. It would have been useless to fight her strong body.

Her spasms came and went. She'd slow down for a moment and then resume her bucking motion. When it appeared that she was in danger of tiring, Doc took over with his plunging hips.

"Hard," she moaned. "As hard as you can. Oh, it feels so good to have you on top of me."

She pulled her legs back, thrusting her crotch forward. Doc

adjusted his own body, keeping his thick cock inside her. She cried out when his hips resumed their rigorous plunges. Doc intended to drive all desire out of her.

Doc abandoned all sense of restraint. His flirtation with Margaret Anderson had left him horny as hell. As he fucked Lorna Wolcott, the vision of his other lady friend came to him. He thought of their kiss in the canyon and the whiteness of her perfect shoulders. His cock swelled with the burst that rose from his testicles. When he came inside her, Mrs. Wolcott grabbed his head and pulled his face down into her breasts.

"Thank you," she moaned. "Thank you."

Doc rolled off her and stretched out next to her buxom frame. He waited for her breathing to subside, hoping she wouldn't fall asleep. Both of them were perspiring heavily. Doc decided that he had enjoyed her, even though he had been acting in the line of duty. Hopefully Miss Anderson had not heard him. She had been hard at work across the hall when Doc had arrived.

"Thank you again," said Lorna Wolcott.

She rolled over toward him. Her breasts flopped onto his chest. Doc stroked her forehead, wondering how deeply she was involved in her husband's scheme.

"Have you lived a long time out here?" Doc asked.

"All my life," she replied. "My father homesteaded north of here. My mother was a Mexican woman. She died when I was ten."

"Is your father still alive?" Doc asked.

"No, he had an accident a while back," she replied. "I guess you saw that I was wearing black at dinner."

"I'm so sorry. How did he die?"

"Fell off a cliff," she replied. "Simon saw the whole thing. I sure miss my daddy. He was a good man."

She started to cry. Doc drew her close to him, kissing her forehead. She misunderstood the gesture and reached for his crotch. Doc started to draw away, but her hand was persistent.

"I want to do it again," she sobbed.

"Well, I don't know."

"I'll get you hard again," she replied. "I'm wet myself. Please, I can do it."

"Well, if you think you're able..."

She was off the bed in a quick movement. Doc heard her rattling around in a drawer of the nightstand next to the bed. In a moment, she was back on the sheets, lying beside him. Doc felt a slippery substance as she grabbed his cock again.

"It comes from the cactus plant," she said. "The Mexican Indians think it will make a man of you. I tried it on Simon but it didn't work."

But Doc felt it working. As she rubbed him with the lotion, he felt his cock expanding. She cupped his testicles with her sticky fingers, rolling them around in her palm. In five minutes she had revived Doc completely.

"I'm going to get on top," she said.

Before Doc could say a word, she had straddled him. Her hands guided his slick cock into position. He felt her weight as she sat down on his penis, holding it deep inside her. She waited for a moment before she started moving her hips. As she pulled the phallus in and out of her, she leaned forward, lowering her sagging breasts into Doc's face.

"I love you, Mr. Weatherbee," she said. "I love to have you inside me."

Doc had never been with woman who talked so much. Nor had he been with a woman so proficient in the ways of love. Lorna closed her eyes as she rolled her hips. A smile was spread across her mouth. Doc was trapped beneath her, having surrendered to her armorous designs. She had said that she liked to talk after making love. As twilight settled in on the dusk window, Doc wondered when *after* would arrive.

CHAPTER TWELVE

Lorna Wolcott had not been lying when she told Doc that she liked to talk after making love. With her warm body next to Doc, she had talked well into the evening, describing a misfortunate life in her hoarse voice. He could not see her face as she spoke, but he was moved by the sincerity in her tone. She had been forced to association with her husband by dire circumstances.

Her father, Liam Pixton, had been a homesteader who came west from Ohio with his first wife. Fever took her, leaving him to marry a Mexican woman, Lorna's mother. Her father was not the greatest of farmers, and in fact they scarcely made a living. When her mother had died of cholera, ten-year-old Lorna had moved into Santa Fe with her father, where Liam Pixton became one of the town drunks. Lorna began taking in laundry and cleaning houses for well-to-do women. No decent man would have anything to do with her—unless they wanted her ripe body. Things had been entirely rough for her until Simon Wolcott arrived in Santa Fe.

She couldn't remember everything about Wolcott's entry into their lives. She didn't even know how Wolcott found out that her father still owned the basin land. But Wolcott had paid the back taxes and had promised to make things better for them, proving his word by moving them into the hacienda ten miles outside Santa Fe.

Simon had asked her to marry him when she was in Dodge City on business with him and her father. She had said yes, and they were hitched when they returned to Santa Fe. It was like a dream come true for her. Simon was a gentleman, not the crude type of man who wanted only one thing. Then she found out on their wedding night that Wolcott had not wanted anything, not even to share a bed. When Lorna pressed him, he had wanted her to do things that did not seem natural. Still, she did them until he lost interest again.

But since her father had taken the fall off the cliff, Simon was all she had. Simon had seen the accident. Her father, against her husband's wishes, had gone into the hills after a mountain lion. Liam Pixton had wanted the skin, Wolcott had said, and he had fallen during pursuit of the trophy. Doc wondered how much help Wolcott had given him—a push, perhaps?

"Was your father much of a hunter?" Doc asked.

"He liked to hunt as much as any man," she replied. "And he had always wanted to kill a mountain lion. He used to talk about it sometimes."

"Did you see the body?" Doc asked.

"No," she replied. "Simon asked the doctor to put down that my father died of natural causes. I agreed. Daddy wouldn't have wanted anyone to know he died by falling off a cliff."

"Where does your husband hail from?" Doc asked.

She raised herself on one elbow, looking into his eyes.

"He comes from San Francisco. Why do you ask?"

Doc touched her forehead. Her eyes were so innocent. He had decided that she was not completely aware of her husband's dealings. She had spoken too freely about situations where complicity demanded silence and discretion. Still, the printer would be able to identify her as the woman who purchased the bogus bills of sale. She was the only link to Wolcott and the false receipts. Doc felt sorry that Lorna Pixton would be dragged into court. He wondered if she would be convicted as an accomplice.

"Why are you asking about my husband?" Lorna asked.

"Well," Doc replied. "He seems to be a very resourceful man. I'm quite intrigued by the idea of investing out here. What sort of business are you involved in?"

"You don't know?" she replied.

"Our department hasn't told us," he said.

"Simon hasn't told me either," she said. "He just keeps saying that we're going to be rich."

"Any hints as to how?"

"He just keeps saying that we're going to feed every Indian in New Mexico and Arizona. I don't know, I guess he has something . . . What's the matter, Mr. Weatherbee?"

Doc sat up quickly. He had heard the rattling of a harness. Simon Wolcott's surrey was rolling between the gates of the hacienda. Doc could see Wolcott through the bedroom window.

"Your husband is home," Doc said, leaping up to find his pants. "You'd better take your leave."

"But he won't—"

"Don't tarry," Doc replied, taking her arm. "And put on your gown before you go into the hall."

"You don't have to worry," she said, pulling the peignoir over her shoulders. "My husband won't . . ."

Doc pulled her to the door. She wrapped her arms around his neck and pressed her breasts into his naked chest. Her mouth sought his for a hasty goodbye kiss.

"I'll be around late tonight."

Doc flung open the door. Poised at the threshold, ready to knock, was Margaret Anderson. She cried out when she saw Lorna Wolcott with her arms around Doc. Doc could not remember when he had seen a more irate woman.

"Tramp!" cried Miss Anderson.

She grabbed Lorna's hair, dragging her into the hall. Doc held on to Lorna's shoulders, trying to pull them apart. But the spinning weight of their bodies slung him down the corridor. He bounced off the stucco wall and tumbled to the floor. As he started to regain his balance, he felt a pair of strong hands under his arms, lifting him to his feet.

"Looks like you got some trouble," Raider said.

"You! But how . . ."

"What's going on here, Mr. Weatherbee?" asked Simon Wolcott.

He had walked up behind Raider and stood looking at the two women as they went at it.

"Nothin' but a jealous woman," Raider replied.

Miss Anderson ripped the peignoir form Lorna's body. Lorna responded by grabbing Miss Anderson's hair. They tumbled to the floor, clawing and screeching.

"I'm terribly sorry, Mr. Wolcott," Doc offered.

"Yes," Wolcott replied dryly.

"Want me to take care of this, sir?" Raider asked.

"Do," Wolcott replied. "And come to my room when you're finished. I want to see that you get paid."

He smiled at Raider and hurried off.

"Where did you come from?" Doc asked.

"Shh, let me separate these two fillies before one of them gets killed," Raider replied.

Lorna had gained the advantage. She was on top of Miss Anderson, who held her wrists to keep Lorna from getting to her eyes. Raider grabbed Lorna to pull her off. When she turned on him, he tapped her on the chin, rendering her unconscious.

"She went out like a candle in a cyclone," Raider said.

"Put her in my room," Doc said.

Miss Anderson came up from the floor, going straight for Doc with her outstretched arms. She wasn't going to hug him. He managed to fend off her blows, finally trapping her in his arms.

"If you don't slow down, I'll have Raider hit you, too," Doc said. "He'd rather enjoy that."

"You said you'd never have anything to do with a woman like that!"

Raider stepped back into the hall before Doc could reply.

"Into Margaret's room," Doc said, dragging Miss Anderson with him.

When they were inside her chamber, Doc let her out of the bear hug. She drew away from him. He grabbed her arm and spun her around.

"I've never questioned your business," Doc said. "How dare you question mine!"

"But you—"

"Pack everything you own," Doc said. "And hurry."

"Do you expect me to obey you?" she cried.

"Only if you value your life," Doc replied.

They stood eye to eye for a fiery moment. Raider laughed. Love was giving Doc a fit. He figured the eastern lady would be a handful for his partner. Miss Anderson broke away and started to roll up her maps. Doc turned back to Raider.

"We're leaving," Doc said. "I wholeheartedly suggest that you come with us."

"I don't think I want to do whatever it is that Wolcott has in mind," Raider replied. "I'll go with you."

"How did you get here?" Doc asked.

"Wolcott is in cahoots with the sheriff. We hooked up with him north of here. He's got cattle penned up."

"That makes sense," Doc said.

"Why?"

"Lorna Wolcott said something about feeding every Indian in this territory. There doesn't seem to be a reservation moving in, so perhaps the connection with the Interior Department has something to do with selling beef to the government."

"Beef for Indians?" Raider asked.

"That basin land would be perfect for a herd. And if there is an option for a reservation site, then Wolcott profits doubly."

"Three times if you count the land swindle," Raider said.

"That's the only thing we'll be able to pin on him," Doc said. "But that will be enough."

"What about the woman?" Doc asked.

"Lorna? Well, the printer can identify her," Doc replied. "I wonder how much she knows in actuality. It's possible that her father was murdered. But she doesn't seem to be the mastermind of the operation. In fact, she seems quite innocent."

"You would say that!" Miss Anderson rasped.

"I think we have enough evidence to seek legal recourse," Doc said, ignoring her.

"Territorial court?" Raider asked.

"Any better suggestions?"

"Not that I can think of."

"So let's move out of here," Doc said. "Are you ready, Margaret?"

She only huffed and puffed as she grappled with her cases. Doc ducked across the hall and gathered the rest of his belongings. Lorna's body was sprawled across the bed. The poor woman, he thought. When he went back into Margaret's room, Raider was opening the window.

"Can't we leave by the door?" Miss Anderson asked.

"We won't be seen this way," Raider replied. "I'll go first."

Miss Anderson's eyes bulged when Raider withdrew the .44 from his holster. Raider slid through the window and dropped on the ground outside. Doc took Miss Anderson's bundles and pushed them through the casement one at a time. When he offered her a boost, she did not refuse. The sight of the pistol had made her considerably calmer.

"The horses are in the stable," Doc said to Raider. "Where's your mount?"

"Same place," he replied. "The Mexican kid took it."

They hurried across the dark yard to the stable. A silver dollar prompted the stable boy to help Doc as he hitched up Judith. Miss Anderson tied her bundles onto the packhorse. Raider helped her with the knots in the dim lantern light. When they were ready, Doc took a deep breath and looked at his partner.

"We're set," he said. "Slow. And no gunplay unless it's absolutely necessary. Margaret, tie your horses to the back of the wagon. You'll ride with me."

"I'd rather die first," she replied.

"You might get your wish, ma'am," Raider replied, thumbing back the hammer of the .44.

She jumped onto the wagon without a word. Raider tied her horses to the back of the Studebaker and climbed into the saddle of the bay gelding. Doc took the reins and urged Judith forward. As they approached the gate, they heard the dogs growling. Then they heard Wolcott's voice cutting through the darkness.

"You're not leaving," he called. "Satan, get them."

Raider saw the blurred movement as the dog rushed toward the wagon. The .44 barked, lighting up the yard with its muzzle flash. Raider hit the dog on the second shot. He heard the yelp and saw the animal fall.

"You wanna be next, Wolcott?" Raider asked.

Wolcott was standing on the veranda of the hacienda. Raider could barely see him, but he knew he didn't have a gun in his hand. The other dog was by his side, growling and ready to attack.

"What is this about?" Wolcott cried, a quavering evident in his voice for the first time.

"It's about a man named Thomas," Raider replied. "About the way you took his money. About the way you're gonna give it back. Doc, take off, I'll cover you."

"Wait, we can talk!" Wolcott cried. "I can make you rich men."

Doc snapped his whip just above Judith's ear. The mule lurched forward. The Mexican boy had run ahead to open the gates. Raider kept his eye on Wolcott until Doc was outside the walls.

"You better not leave the territory," Raider cried. "If you do, I'll find you, Wolcott. I'll personally string you up. You here me, boy?"

"You're a dead man, Tatum!"

Raider wheeled the gelding and sprinted between the gates to catch up with Doc.

They returned to the ravine to find the Thomas family in good spirits. Calvin Thomas had recovered fully and was determined to help in bringing Wolcott to justice. He also vowed revenge on the sheriff, a move that Doc tried to temper with reason. Wolcott would be their first target. They would get the money back and then try to get the sheriff on attempted murder and conspiracy.

The most unexpected find was the presence of one Olie Biernson, a Swede whom Thomas had found on the plain, wandering about aimlessly. He carried a bill of sale from the Hutchison Western Title Company signed by Wilson Samuels. Although he did not speak much English, Doc managed to ascertain that he had been swindled in the same scheme by a man who matched Wolcott's description.

"Looks like we got ourselves a good court case," Raider said.

"I hope so," Thomas replied.

"Everything fits," Doc said. "With our findings and testimony, I daresay the court will not overlook your complaint. However, I suggest we report immediately to the marshal in Santa Fe. We want Wolcott arrested before he runs."

"He won't run," Raider replied. "And if he does, I'll get him myself."

Raider ignored the way Lucy Thomas was staring at him. He turned to Miss Anderson, who had become rather sullen. It was something to see Doc having trouble with a woman.

"You goin' back to Santa Fe, miss?" Raider asked.

"Yes, I suppose so," she replied.

"Maybe you could help these folks here get settled. I think

they should all come, don't you, Doc?"

"Yes," Doc replied. "If they can't find a dwelling, then they can make camp just outside of town. There should be a sentry on duty around the clock."

"Don't worry," said Calvin Thomas. "I'll see to it that that white man pays for what he did to us."

"I assure you he will pay," Doc replied. "But leave that to us. And the territorial court."

Suddenly they were all quiet. Only the babbling of the stream resounded through the ravine. They warmed themselves by the fire, waiting for the sun to rise so they could start for Santa Fe.

CHAPTER THIRTEEN

The next afternoon Simon Wolcott was arrested without incident by a reluctant and apologetic marshal. Wolcott, playing the pillar of the community, quietly posted bail money and then returned to his hacienda. Doc was surprised that Wolcott had not made more fuss about his arrest. He had learned enough about the man to know that he was not to be underestimated. In answer to Doc's doubts, the marshal promised to have a deputy keep an eye on the hacienda to make sure Wolcott didn't run.

"That was easy enough," Raider said.

"Yes, too easy," Doc replied. "I wonder what Wolcott has up his sleeve?"

"He can't keep dodgin' the truth forever," Raider said.

"Perhaps not. Or maybe he's counting on the color of our client's skin to assure him a victory in court."

The Thomas family had camped on the edge of town in a stand of cottonwood trees. Doc and Raider decided to stay with them, as did the Swede. Margaret Anderson retired to a hotel in Santa Fe without so much as a word to Doc. If Doc was upset, he did not show it. Instead, he penned a report about their findings and then headed for the telegraph office.

In a wire to the home office, Doc reported that they were taking the case to trial. A reply came back, directing them to seek out James Hauck, attorney-at-law. Hauck was a young red-haired man with searching blue eyes. He had come from Illinois to find new opportunities in Santa Fe. Allan Pinkerton had been a friend of his late father. Doc and Raider brought Thomas and his brother to the small office. Hauck was surprised by the arrival of the Pinkertons and their two Negro clients.

"You say Mr. Pinkerton sent you?" he asked.

Doc explained the land scheme and presented the two fake bills of sale given to Thomas and the Swede. He then explained the route of their investigation and the way they had arrived at their conclusions. Calvin Thomas insisted on interjecting his tale of the run-in with the sheriff. They let him speak his piece and then turned back to the evidence.

"The printer will have to be summoned from Dodge City," Hauck said, leaning back in his chair. "The evidence is strong in our client's favor. I'll petition the court for a trial date. Will you send the wire to Dodge City, Mr. Weatherbee?"

"Of course."

Hauck turned his gaze on Alexander Othello Thomas. Thomas seemed content to take the legal recourse. Hauck hesitated before he spoke.

"I must say one thing, Mr. Thomas. Are you aware that a jury might find in favor of Wolcott because he's a white man?"

"You mean because I am a colored man," Thomas replied.

"Yes," Hauck said. "We have to consider that."

"What can be done?" Doc asked.

"I suggest we argue the case in front of a judge," Hauck replied. "Waive the right to jury trial."

"Very well," Thomas replied.

"Judge Miller is a good man," Hauck said. "I've never known him to hand down an unfair verdict."

"Let's pray for a just decision," Thomas replied.

"I also think it would be wise to get statements from anyone who saw Wolcott in Dodge City," Hauck said. "The printer can bring them with him."

"This boy's thinkin'," Raider said.

"What about the sheriff?" asked Calvin Thomas. "Are we just going to let him go free?"

"No," Hauck replied. "But that will be another case entirely. I suggest we recover your money before we do anything else."

"Agreed," Thomas said.

"No. That white bastard shot me," Calvin cried. "I'll kill him myself if I have to."

"We wait, little brother," Thomas said. "These men have helped us so far. We'll seek justice in the proper—"

"White man's justice?" Calvin cried.

"White man's justice," Thomas replied.

They were silent as the younger man's temper settled. Thomas then withdrew a leather purse from his coat jacket. He stacked five double eagles together and put them on Hauck's desk.

"Will this retain your services?" Thomas asked.

"For several months," Hauck replied.

"Then I will see you in court," Thomas said.

Raider glanced at his partner. Doc was sitting in his chair, his hands locked over his lap. Usually when they wrapped up a case, Doc lit up a cigar to celebrate. Usually he was satisfied with himself. But he seemed slightly uneasy this time.

"You spooked about something?" Raider asked as they headed back to camp.

"No, not really," Doc replied. "Unless you count Wolcott's penchant for surprises."

"It don't matter, Doc," Raider said. "Hell, everything is legal. Just like you like it. What can go wrong, Doc? Wolcott knows he's got his balls in a bear trap."

"I hope you're right, my friend. I hope you're right."

Late April snow began to fall on trial day. A spring blizzard swept down out of the north, dumping wet flakes on everything. Doc gazed out of his hotel room window at the mushy streets. He had taken the room to be near the witness, Harlan Huckleby. The printer from Dodge City was the only one who could link the phony bills of sale to the Wolcotts. Huckleby was staying across the street at the marshal's office. He had come in the night before on the stage. Everything was progressing as planned.

Raider had refused the hotel, preferring to stay over the livery with Thomas and the Swede. Margaret Anderson, who was still not talking to Doc, had moved the rest of the Thomas family into a rented house in the Mexican section of town. It was old and dilapidated, but there was plenty of room. The Indian girl was never far from Thomas's side. They had been keeping Raider awake over the livery. After a week of waiting for the judge to hear the case, everyone was ready to get it finished.

At eight o'clock in the morning on trial day, Doc roused Raider, Thomas, and the Swede from the livery. They trekked through the snow to James Hauck's office, where they met the young lawyer with a law book under his arm. Together they walked to the section of town where Margaret Anderson and the Thomas women were staying. The women had prepared a hearty breakfast.

"Good hotcakes, Mrs. Thomas," said James Hauck to Beatrice.

After that they ate in silence. Raider hated it when everyone was jumpy-like. His own stomach wouldn't accept anything but a cup of black coffee.

"What the hell's wrong around here?" Raider barked. "Ain't no need for ever'body to be so jumpy."

Calvin Thomas knocked his plate away, startling the lawyer.

"What if Wolcott don't show?" Calvin cried. "What if they just say, 'These niggers is lyin'?' What if they just laugh at us?"

Hauck swallowed a lump of hotcake. "I assure you that he will show, Calvin. If he doesn't, he loses by default."

"Why? 'Cause my brother paid some white lawyer? 'Cause we paid you some gold? That gold ain't been nothin' but trouble."

"Shut up, boy!" Thomas cried.

"You have to hold your temper in court," said James Hauck.

"Maybe he oughta stay here," Raider said.

"I've had a belly full of you, cracker!" Calvin said.

Raider stood up, knocking his chair to the wooden floor. Calvin's eyes were burning. Raider leaned across the table and put a finger in his face.

"You been lookin' for someone to whip your ass since we started this trial thing," Raider said. "If you shit this thing up, where's your brother gonna be? Huh?"

Calvin looked like he wanted to come up out of the chair. Raider would have taken it to him, Doc thought. Thomas leaned and put his hand on his brother's shoulder.

"The man's right," Thomas said. "Stay here, Calvin. We'll send someone for you if we need you."

"Yeah, I'll stay," Calvin snarled. "I don't want no justice from the white man."

He left the table and went out in back of the house. James

Hauck shook his head, trying to regain his concentration. The women were nervous and silent. Doc glared at Raider.

"What'd I do?" Raider asked.

"Nothing out of the ordinary," Doc replied. "Just your usual lack of brains and decorum."

"The kid had it coming," Raider said.

"Forget it, Raider," Thomas replied. "Mr. Hauck, it's quarter to nine. Shall we go?"

They trudged back through the falling snow. A cold wind swept down, freezing the flakes into icy layers. Raider hated spring snow. It was hell on his boots.

In spite of the snow a crowd had gathered in front of the courthouse. Doc saw the printer being escorted through the mob by the marshal. A huge turnout was not surprising. The local newspaper had whipped up a frenzy among the pro-Wolcott townspeople.

"There's the nigger," someone cried.

They rushed them, forcing Doc and Raider to shield Thomas. When they pushed through the courthouse door, the mob filed in behind them, filling the gallery. Hauck and Thomas went through a scrolled gate to sit at the plaintiff's desk. Doc and Raider found a place next to the Swede in the third row of the gallery.

"Where's Wolcott?" Raider asked.

"He has ten minutes to get here," Doc replied. "Would you like to wager on his entrance?"

"What if he don't show?" Raider asked.

"I've felt strangely all along," Doc replied. "If he . . ."

The crowd cheered behind them. Wolcott strode into the courtroom clad in a fancy suit. Behind him walked a neatly dressed balding man and an army officer in full formal dress. Thomas stood when he saw the two men behind Wolcott. The army officer, a colonel, smiled at Thomas.

"What's goin' on?" Raider asked.

"Wolcott is up to something," Doc replied. "Look at him smiling like an eel."

Thomas jumped over the railing and started toward the door. The army officer stepped in his way, extending a friendly hand. But Thomas brushed him aside, bolting for the exit. Several members of the gallery followed him, blocking Doc and Raider's path. When someone cried, "The nigger's runnin'!" the courtroom erupted in chaos.

"The back door," Raider cried to Doc.

They fought their way through the crowd. Doc followed Raider over the rail, through the back, past the baffled judge. Outside, they ran down an alley to the main street. Raider half expected to see a lynch mob, but Thomas was nowhere in sight. A group of men stood in front of the courthouse, patting Simon Wolcott on the back.

They found Thomas huddled with his family in the run-down house. He was sitting at the kitchen table, staring down at the floor. The Indian girl had her hands on his shoulders. Miss Anderson stood with Lucy and Beatrice. Calvin Thomas was shouting at his older brother.

"I said it wasn't no use," he cried. "They done took it all. Now we ain't got nothin'!"

Thomas just sat there, taking it in. Raider thought he looked like a sick prairie dog. Something had gotten to him.

"Why'd you run?" Raider asked.

Thomas would not look at him.

"This has something to do with you finding that gold, doesn't it?" Doc asked.

Thomas sighed. "Correct, Mr. Weatherbee."

"You lost me," Raider said.

"The army officer . . . he was your former commander, wasn't he?" Doc asked.

Thomas nodded. "The other man was a gold dealer," he said. "I traded Red Wolf's gold for double eagles. It appears that we are surprised whether we like it or not, gentlemen."

"You ran because you took that gold?" Raider asked.

"Don't you understand?" Thomas cried. "I would have to explain in court where I got the gold that bought the basin land. And if I didn't tell the truth, they'd simply ask the gold dealer what I traded to him for the gold pieces. Wolcott must have figured out what I had done. He brought my commanding officer here, knowing that I wouldn't testify with him watching. I could never let him know that I took Red Wolf's gold. I'd face shame, possibly even prosecution."

"My brother's white pride!" Calvin shouted.

Thomas slammed his fists on the table.

"Shut up, Calvin!" he cried.

"I told you it wasn't nothin' but trouble," Calvin persisted. "But you had a head full of dreams. The West, where a black man has a chance. Where's our chance, brother?"

Thomas went after his brother, swinging wildly, forcing the ladies to scatter. Raider grabbed Thomas before he landed any damaging blows. Doc stepped between them, pushing Calvin backward.

"Look at the both of you," Doc cried. "You're flesh and blood. If you don't stick together, we're never going to get out of this."

"We can't get out!" Calvin said.

"I have a plan," Doc replied.

Calvin glared at him. The women looked at him too. Raider grinned for effect.

"Listen to Doc," Raider said. "He's got more tricks than a otter playin' with a gator's tail."

"He ain't gonna do nothin'," Calvin said. "How's he gonna get the white man without us goin' to court?"

"By catching him in the act," Doc replied. "But I must have complete cooperation. Especially from you, Calvin. If you don't give me another chance, then you really have lost everything. I'm your last hope, son."

Calvin kicked a chair. "All right," he replied. "I'll listen, damn it. But if you don't convince me, there'll be one dead white man before morning. And when I'm finished with Wolcott, I'll go after that cracker sheriff."

"I assure you, that won't be necessary," Doc replied. "Now, if you'll gather around the table, gentlemen."

"What you got in mind, Doc?" Raider asked.

"Well," he replied. "The first thing we have to do is head back to the basin."

CHAPTER FOURTEEN

"Looks like the Chinaman has settled in pretty good," Raider said. "Big family. Eight of them."

Doc, Raider, and Calvin were situated on a high rift in the forest, looking down on the snow-covered basin. Calvin had found the jutting ledge by following a deer trail that began at the wall of the ravine where they had camped again. Raider held Doc's telescope to his eye, looking down at the Chinese family. Doc had remembered seeing them before with Wolcott. Now their tents were pitched on the ground of the basin. If Wolcott pulled his swindle again, they would bring another complaint and nail him cold.

"Two days," Raider said. "No sheriff yet. Wolcott may be waiting for the kettle to cool."

"Can't get much colder," Calvin rejoined.

"At least it stopped snowing," Raider said.

"For how long?" Calvin asked.

"Hand me the glass," Doc said.

Raider gave him the telescope and folded his arms over his chest. Doc looked down at the encampment. Raider wanted to go back to the cave and warm his hands by the fire.

"See anything, Doc?" Calvin asked.

"Not yet," Doc replied. "Our friends in the basin are celebrating. Do you hear them chanting?"

"Maybe one of us should go back to the cave," Raider offered.

"All right," Doc replied. "Why don't you go, Calvin?"

"Sure," he said blankly.

Doc made an effort to include Calvin in their watches on the ledge. It gave Calvin a sense of self-importance and allowed Doc to keep an eye on him at the same time. Calvin followed the path back through the trees. Raider slapped his arms.

"You coulda sent me back," he said.

"What? And miss all your delightful conversation?"

Raider grunted. "What makes you so sure Wolcott is gonna run these people out of here?"

"He's a hungry serpent," Doc replied. "And he has to act soon."

"He mentioned somethin' about expectin' someone to take a look at the land," Raider said.

"Exactly," Doc replied. "He has to rid himself of these settlers before the wheels begin to turn. This is his last roll of the dice. One too many chances, I'm betting."

"Aw, hell."

Light snow had begun to fall again. Doc and Raider shivered on the ledge, keeping an eye on the tents below. Strange, lilting chimes were making music in the basin. Raider wished he was in bed with Claire.

"You got anythin' warm to drink?" Raider asked.

"No, I don't," Doc replied. "If you want . . . did you hear that?"

Crunching footsteps in the fresh snow above them. Raider brought out the .44 and thumbed back the hammer. Thomas and the Indian girl came down the path.

"Just us," Thomas said. "I saw Calvin on the trail."

"You got any applejack?" Raider said, holstering his pistol.

"Some," Thomas replied.

"Hell, break it out!" Raider cried.

They passed a small bottle between them. The girl drank too. As she lowered the bottle from her lips, she looked out over the basin. Her eyes narrowed and she spoke in her own language.

"She says a wagon is coming," Thomas said.

"I don't see nothin'," Raider said. "Besides, she can't see in this snow."

Doc raised the telescope, searching the basin through the veil of falling crystals. A covered wagon lumbered over the plain like a lost spring beetle. Doc handed the glass to Raider.

"Do you see it?" Doc asked. "Perhaps a half mile away from the tents. They're almost on the Chinese family."

"Looks like the sheriff and his boy Shorty," Raider replied. "He snuck up on us in this snowfall."

"Why do they need a wagon?" Doc asked.

"Devil take 'em," Raider cried, dropping the telescope from his eye. "I know what he's got in that wagon. A goddamn Gatling gun."

"We have to get down there," Thomas said.

"The sheriff is too close," Doc replied. "We'd never make it down in time. Let's hope the Chinaman goes peaceably."

Raider watched the whole thing through the telescope. The sheriff parked the wagon in front of the tents. A Chinese man, the head of the family, came out to meet Bridge. They argued when the sheriff flashed some papers at him. The Chinese man waved a knife. Bridge drew on him and shot him in the chest.

Shorty hurried as he rolled back the wagon cover. Raider saw the Gatling gun that had been mounted on the wagon bed. The rest of the family came out of the tents to see their fallen patriarch. Shorty turned the handle of the Gatling. The revolving battery cut the family to ribbons in an instant. The echo seemed to last forever.

"My God," Thomas cried.

"We've got to go after those bastards," Raider said.

"We can't charge the Gatling gun," Doc replied. "They have to bury those bodies. We'll get them on the trail."

"I don't believe it," Raider cried. "Look!"

"Calvin!" Thomas cried.

His younger brother had burst out of the forest on Raider's gelding. Apparently he had heard the shots and had gone out to investigate. He opened up on the sheriff with the Henry rifle, but it was a futile gesture. The Gatling cut a trail to his chest, knocking him to the ground.

They could only sit and watch the sheriff's treachery. Bridge and his associate started loading the bodies into the back of the wagon. When their task was done, they went back in the direction they had come from.

"I won't let them bury my brother," Thomas said softly.

"We won't have any trouble following them in the snow," Raider cried. "Bastards!"

"Horrid," Doc rejoined.

"Let's get started," Thomas said.

He was full of hatred. But Raider understood. He felt the same way.

They followed the sheriff's path all night. He was heading back to Raton at a slow pace. Doc guided Judith along, while Thomas and Raider were forced to mount the two horses from Thomas's team. Just before dawn they stopped at the bottom of the main street. The covered wagon was parked next to the sheriff's office, blocking the small office window. Bridge had not stopped along the road to bury the bodies.

"Whatta ya think, Doc?" Raider asked.

"We can wait and surprise them," Doc replied. "Or we can call them out and take our chances."

"There's only two of them," Raider replied. "I say we call them out. I can get behind them barrels on the porch of the general store. You stay down here with my rifle. Thomas, you can back up Doc."

"So I'm still nothing but a buffalo soldier."

"Well, there ain't no need for you to be killed too," Raider said.

"No, I suppose not."

"Okay, Doc," Raider said, checking the cylinder of his .44. "Here I go. Shoot straight if it gets hot."

Raider ran low for the porch of the general store. The snow had stopped again, but the ground was thoroughly covered. Raider was worried that the sheriff might hear his feet in the crisp, frozen layers. When he reached the general store, he took a quick turn down the alley to make sure the sheriff wasn't sleeping. Bridge's room was empty. Raider went back to the porch and slipped behind a barrel of beans.

"Bridge!" he called. "Come out of there. We saw you kill those Chinamen and we're takin' you in for it!"

No reply from Bridge. Below, Doc was ready with the Winchester. He didn't see Thomas slip away behind him. Instead, he drew a bead on the door to the office.

"Hear me, Bridge?" Raider called. "Come peaceable and there won't be no shootin'!"

"That you, Pinkerton?" Bridge replied.

"We got you flat," Raider cried. "Give it up."

"I'm comin' out, Pinkerton," Bridge replied. "Don't shoot."

Raider kept his eyes on the door. The sheriff came out with both hands in the air. He started toward Raider, who didn't move from behind the barrels.

"Stop it right there," Raider said. "Turn around and walk toward Doc, slow-like. Doc, you stay down till he gets there."

Bridge pivoted on his heels and started down toward Doc.

"Yeah, you're mighty smart, Pinkerton," Bridge said. "Mighty smart. But you know something? You're still gonna die. Shorty, now!"

The sheriff dived into the snow. The Gatling erupted through the canvas of the wagon, laying down fire on the barrels in front of Raider. Raider couldn't even get off a shot. The Gatling had him pinned. Doc's rifle barked from below, but it was no good. The little man was hidden safely behind the cases of ammunition. The Gatling kicked up dirt down the middle of the street, pinning Doc as well.

"That little son of a bitch climbed out the window," Raider cried.

"Git gone, Pinkertons," the sheriff cried. "We won't do nothin' if you just leave."

"Is that why you killed the Chinamen?" Raider cried. "Because they wouldn't leave?"

"Kill them, Shorty," the sheriff cried. "Plug them good!"

But the Gatling was silent.

"I said to kill them, damn it!"

The canvas dropped away from the wagon. Shorty fell out with his throat slit from ear to ear. Thomas took his place behind the Gatling gun. He swung it around and pointed it at the sheriff.

"No!" Raider cried. "Thomas, don't!"

Snow and dirt mixed where the slugs dug into the ground. The sheriff fell. Raider waited a moment before he moved from behind the barrels. He ran down the street to the spot where Bridge was dying. The Gatling slugs had cut him up pretty badly. Blood was oozing into the slush.

"He's had it," Raider called. "Come on up, Doc. Hey, good work, Thomas. But you shouldn't have . . ."

Raider looked back to see Thomas carrying his brother's body away from the wagon. Doc and Raider followed him into the woods, helping with the shallow grave. When Calvin Thomas was in the ground, Raider covered the moist earth with stones.

"Wolcott must be stopped," Thomas said. "I'll go to court. I'll testify this time."

"I ran into a wire south of here," Raider said. "Maybe Doc ought to send a message to the marshal in Santa Fe."

"No, I'll send a wire to the home office," Doc replied. "Then they can notify the Justice Department that we're going after Wolcott. The marshal would only think we're crying wolf again."

"We'll get him this time," Raider said.

"I'll go with Doc," Thomas said. "Just in case Bridge has any more men in the area."

"When you bury the other bodies, Raider, make sure you look for the false bill of sale. I'm sure Wolcott gave them one," Doc said.

Raider didn't like the idea of burying all the corpses, but he didn't grumble out loud. He was feeling sorry for Thomas, even though he felt the black man had brought on most of his own trouble.

"We got company," Raider said as they walked out of the trees.

A few of the town's citizens had gathered around to witness the results of the shoot-out. Some of them were looking into the wagon where the slaughtered family lay. Raider wondered how much he would have to pay to get one or two of them to help him put the bodies in the ground.

Thomas was sullen as he rode next to Doc on the wagon seat. Doc offered him a cheroot and both men smoked. A light rain had begun to fall instead of the snow. The air was warmer. Doc hoped the wires had held up in the blizzard.

Ten miles south of Raton, Thomas climbed the pole to hook up the wires. He came back down and stood behind Doc, who wrapped the copper ends around the telegraph key terminals. Then he took out a piece of paper to write out his message.

"If the wires held, I'll be able to ... unhh ..."

The lights went out of Doc's head. He fell forward, slumping unconsciously over the telegraph key. Thomas had hit him from behind with a small stone.

"Sorry, Doc," Thomas said. "But I have to settle up with Wolcott myself. I should have done it a long time ago."

Doc stirred an hour later to see that Thomas had fled on Judith, riding her bareback. There was nothing to do but follow the trail back to Raton. Doc had been walking two hours before he saw Raider coming toward him on horseback.

"What the hell, Doc?"

"Thomas left me," Doc replied. "I'll give you one guess as to where he's going."

"Wolcott?"

"Correct," Doc said. "He's got about three hours on us. I just hope we can catch him before he does something stupid."

"Yeah, I guess so," Raider replied. "But would it be a crime if he did kill Wolcott?"

Doc shook his head and climbed into the saddle behind Raider. Doc didn't even want to think about the consequences of Thomas's bold move. He just wanted to reach Wolcott's hacienda as quickly as possible.

CHAPTER FIFTEEN

The light rain had stopped again when Doc and Raider arrived at Wolcott's hacienda. They searched the house until they found Lorna Wolcott lying unconscious in her husband's bedroom. Doc picked her up and put her on the feather mattress, examining her for bruises. Raider's eyes were trained on the opening in her robe.

"If you're through gawking, get some water," Doc said.

Raider hurried down the hall, looking for the kitchen. But there was no water pump next to the sink, so he had to go outside to the well. As he stepped through the back door, his feet stumbled over a furry carcass on the stoop. Wolcott's other dog was lying dead on the ground. Thomas had got him one, Raider thought. He filled a wooden bucket at the well and went back to the bedroom. Doc wet his handkerchief and dabbed it on Mrs. Wolcott's forehead.

"She still with us?" Raider asked.

"The poor woman," Doc replied. "I'd say she passed out from fright. Here, she's coming around."

Lorna Wolcott screamed and then opened her brown eyes. She sat up abruptly and threw her arms around Doc. He let her cry it out and then pushed her gently away.

"Lorna, you have to tell us what happened," he said softly.

"The black man," she cried. "He came out of nowhere, like the Devil."

She described how the dog had started barking out back, how Simon had gone to investigate, how he had commanded the dog to attack Thomas. When she heard the snarling, she looked out the window to see the black man strangling the dog with his bare hands. When Thomas threw the dog to the ground, her husband had shot at him twice with a small-caliber derringer.

"I don't think he hit him," she said. "The black man just kept coming. He wasn't human. He caught Simon and beat him until he was knocked out. Then he tied him over a horse and rode out of here on a mule. There was nothing I could do."

"I know," Doc said. "Raider, see if you can find some whiskey."

Raider found a bottle of brandy in a desk that rested in a corner of the room. A sheaf of papers had been stacked together on the desk top. Raider poured Mrs. Wolcott a drink and then called Doc to the desk. Doc shifted through the papers and nodded.

"Wolcott was trying to get the government to buy his cattle," Doc said. "A representative of the Interior Department is due next month."

"He ain't gonna get much of nothin' if Thomas has him," Raider replied.

"He'll have to go back to the ravine to get his family," Doc said.

"You think he's killed him yet?"

Doc did not reply. He gazed out the window instead. Clouds were gathering on the horizon, behind the mountains. More snow or rain, he thought.

"We have a few hours of light left," Doc said. "I don't know if we can make it before dark."

"I say we ride anyway."

"Who'll stay with me?" asked Lorna Wolcott.

Doc sat on the bed and handed her his .38 Diamondback.

"You'll be safe," he said. "But take this just in case. Get the servants to stay with you. They're probably hiding in the stable after all the commotion."

She grabbed his hands and squeezed them tightly.

"I'm afraid, Mr. Weatherbee."

"The worst is over," Doc said.

"For *you* at least," Raider added in a cold voice that Doc thought he could live without.

*   *   *

The threat of rain was hovering over the Sangre de Cristo ranges in the distance. The remains of a setting sun diffused through the thick clouds. On fresh mounts from Wolcott's stable, Doc and Raider pounded the melting snow on the basin floor. Raider looked up toward the snow-capped peaks above the tree line. Rain was falling at the higher elevations. If Thomas and his family were still in the ravine, they might be in trouble.

Drops of heavy rain rolled down the slopes as they tied their horses in the trees. They had made good time on the fresh animals. If Wolcott was still alive, they might be able to talk Thomas into handing him over. They ran down the path to the streambed that led back into the ravine. But the stream was gone and in its place flowed a white-water rapid. A thunderclap sounded again in the dark sky overhead.

"That snow's melting," Raider said. "Feel the air. Warm again. If Thomas and his family are in there..."

"We can't navigate this stream," Doc said. "The water will crush us if we try to head up that fissure."

"We got one last chance," Raider said.

"I'm listening."

"Go up top, on the trail," Raider said. "Maybe get a rope down to them. That is if they're still alive."

"Do you think they're still in there?"

Raider pointed to the wagon that had been parked in the trees. Judith was also tied nearby, along with another mount from Wolcott's stable. Doc shook his head.

"Damn his stupid hide," he said.

"We need rope," Raider said. "See if Thomas has any in his wagon. God, I wish the rain would stop."

Thunder reminded him that it would not let up. They gathered all of the rope from their saddles and from the wagon. When all of it was tied together, they had about two hundred feet.

"I hope it's enough," Doc said.

"It by God better be."

They climbed through the trees to the path that ran along the ridge to the edge of the ravine. Raider looked down toward the cave where they had camped before. Water had risen about five feet up the ravine wall, almost to the mouth of the cave. In the diminishing light, he could see the torchlight that burned inside the recess.

"Thomas!" he cried.

His voice was barely audible over the river's roar. Raider's hands were trembling as the thunder resounded from above. Pressure was building as the rain melted the snow. If everything flowed steady, the water would rise gradually. But if any of it got trapped, then it might break away all at once. A flash flood was one of the few things that really scared Raider. He took out his .44 and fired into the air.

"What are you doing?" Doc said.

"Thomas has got to hear us," he replied.

Raider fired at the entrance to the cave, knocking bits of rock down into the water. Thomas finally stuck his head out. Doc and Raider shouted and waved furiously. Thomas ducked back into the cave.

"He saw us," Raider said.

"Do you think so?"

"Look, he's waving the torch!"

Thomas wanted out of there. The water was starting to rise into the cave. Raider strained to see if Wolcott was with him. He counted five heads at the cave entrance—Thomas, his sisters, the Indian girl, and another man. Wolcott was alive.

"We've got to get the rope to them," Doc said.

"I think I got a way," Raider replied. "I need a piece of wood that will float."

The rain was steady as Raider tied the loop around the end of a small, thick log. He walked up the ledge about twenty yards and tossed the log out into the current. As the log floated downstream, Raider let out the line, watching as the piece of wood floated toward the other side of the ravine. Thomas hovered at the edge of the cave, reaching out toward the tether. He missed it the first time. The log floated toward the fissure at the mouth of the ravine.

"Pull it up," Doc said. "If you let it get into those rocks we'll never—"

"Shut up, Doc!"

Raider retrieved the line like he was hauling up a Louisiana catfish. He went a little farther up the ledge to where the stream was narrow. Again he tossed out the log and fed the line between his hands. The log shifted in the current, finally catching in a whirling eddy that moved it along the opposite side of the ravine. Raider followed the movement of the wood, feeding out line to keep it on the other bank. As the line neared the cave, Raider held only the frayed end of the tether.

"Come on," he muttered. "Come on."

He saw Thomas in the torchlight. He was using his Henry rifle to reach for the line. Raider felt the rope go tight as Thomas pulled it into the cave.

"One at a time!" Raider cried. "And leave the log tied on!"

Doc joined him in securing the lifeline. The rope bounced up and down as one of the trapped party fixed it around a waist. Thomas tugged on the line to signal that he was ready. Doc and Raider started to pull. Beatrice Thomas, Calvin's widow, swung out into the stream. The current carried her toward the rocky fissure.

"Damn it, Doc, pull harder!"

They pulled her to their side of the raging water before she was swept down into the fissure.

"Heave to," Raider said.

They hoisted her up the ravine wall. She was shivering and exhausted. Raider moved down the ledge, repeating the same procedure for Lucy Thomas and the Indian girl. Lucy threw her arms around Raider's neck, crying for him to save her brother before the white man hurt him.

Raider floated the log down the river again. As the line neared the cave entrance, he could see the two men struggling in the torchlight. Wolcott pushed Thomas into the frothing stream. Then he reached for the line but missed as it swung by him. Raider cursed Wolcott, but then felt tension on the rope. He pulled it toward him, joined by Doc and the women. Together they dragged Thomas to safety.

"Wolcott next," Raider said.

"Leave him to drown," Thomas replied.

"You wanna be like him?" Raider asked.

"We must save him," Doc rejoined, "if only for the gallows."

As Raider started down the ledge, he heard a loud crashing in the slopes above. It sure as hell didn't sound like thunder. Something had given way up top and now it was rolling down the natural channel of the mountain slope. Raider floated the line out into the current. Wolcott dived for the line as it came by. Raider felt the weight as he started to pull. The others helped as he hauled Wolcott toward them.

"He should have tied the rope around him," Doc said. "If he wanted to . . . My God! Raider!"

A wave of rushing water crashed down the ravine like the violent hand of Heaven. The flood wash rounded the bend with an unexpected tidal crush. Wolcott hung on the end of the line in midstream. The water engulfed him as the others held onto the rope. They were almost drawn into the torrent below by the force of the current. Then the line went limp and they hauled in a frayed end.

"He's gone," Raider said. "We tried."

Thomas stood looking down at the water for a moment. Then he put his arm around the Indian girl's shoulder and started down through the forest. Lucy and Beatrice followed him.

"You want to wait until morning and look for the body?" Raider asked.

"We have other business," Doc replied.

They followed the others. It would be futile to look for the body while the water still raged below. They would let the marshal search for the broken remains of Simon Wolcott.

EPILOGUE

"Hello, Mrs. Wolcott," Doc said.

He stood in the doorway of the hacienda, flanked by Raider and the Thomas family.

"What are you doing?" Lorna cried. "And what are they doing here? My God, you're all wet."

"We came to pay our respects to the widow," Raider said.

"Widow?" Lorna replied. "But . . ."

"I'm afraid your husband is no longer with us," Doc replied. "He had unfortunate accident. Just like your father."

"Accident! I'll bet that darkie killed him," she cried, her eyes tearless.

"Mr. Thomas did not kill anyone," Doc replied. "In fact, all of us were near the ravine discussing a land deal when your husband lost his footing and fell to his death. Isn't that how our report will read, Raider?"

"That's the way I saw it, Doc."

"And Lorna, I wouldn't be calling your new business partner by anything but his proper name," Doc said.

"Business partner?" she asked.

"Yes," Doc replied. "You see, unbeknownst to you, your husband was involved in a number of unsavory schemes. However, despite his lack of ethics, he actually maneuvered himself into at least one lawful undertaking, that being the sale of a herd of cattle to the United States government."

"I don't understand," she said.

"Of course not," Doc replied. "Because your husband kept you in the dark. Unless you want to take responsibility for the eight bodies that my partner buried in Raton."

"Hell yeah," Raider rejoined. "You never know what the marshal might say. He might hold you responsible, lady."

"Of course, if Raider and I were to vouch for you, then you might be able to make amends with the people your husband wronged," Doc said.

"And to vouch for me, I have to take this man as my partner?" she asked.

"Yes. Mr. Thomas, his family, and a Swedish gentleman, if he can still be found," Doc replied. "Together, all of you will help to feed every Indian in New Mexico and Arizona."

"Why the hell should I?" she said, grinning.

"Because Simon killed your father, just as he killed that Chinese family," Doc replied. "Just as he would have killed Thomas here if it had been necessary."

"I don't believe you," she said, no longer smiling.

"Lorna," Doc replied softly. "Think about it. Wasn't it too convenient the way your father died? Simon killed him to have him out of the way."

Tears pooled in her brown eyes. Doc moved toward her and took her hands. She fell onto his chest, sobbing. Beatrice and Lucy began to cry too.

"We're gonna have another flood with all this bawling," Raider said. "What'll it be, Lorna?"

"All right," she replied. "All right. I never wanted to hurt anyone. I'll share everything."

"I'll make arrangements with a Mr. Hauck," Doc said. "He's a lawyer in Santa Fe."

"Will you stay with me, Mr. Weatherbee?" Lorna asked.

"I'm afraid I can't," Doc replied. "However, my partner here may be available to stay around to make sure everything moves along smoothly."

"Er, sure, Doc," Raider said, replacing Doc at Lorna's side. "Where you goin' anyways?"

"I have another appointment," Doc replied. "I'm going to ride Judith back to where we left the wagon and then I'm heading for Santa Fe."

As he headed for the door, Alexander Othello Thomas stepped in front of him. Thomas was smiling for the first time since his brother's death. He was one of the most interesting men that Doc had ever met. Doc would always think of him as the buffalo soldier.

"I'd like to shake your hand, sir," Thomas said.

Doc locked hands with him.

"Thank you for everything, Mr. Weatherbee," Thomas said. "You're a true gentleman. Raider, too."

"Hell, Thomas," Raider said. "We're just doing our job. We're Pinkertons."

"If nothing else," Doc replied. "If nothing else."

The next morning, Doc found Miss Anderson waiting at the stage depot in Santa Fe. He sauntered up the wooden sidewalk, dressed in the finest new suit that could be found in the New Mexico Territory. When she looked at him, he tipped his pearl gray derby. She smiled and looked away.

"Hello, Margaret," he said.

"Good day, Mr. Weatherbee," she replied curtly.

Doc leaned against the railing along the sidewalk.

"I thought you'd like to know that we restored the Thomas family to their claim on the basin land," he said.

When she looked at him, her eyes danced in the bright morning sun. The rain had moved south, leaving the skies clear. The ground was still muddy, but the air was warm.

"I'm so pleased to hear that," she said. "Although I never had any doubts that you would."

"I'm sure the inclement weather has delayed the stage," Doc said. "The muddy roads will throw it off schedule."

"I intend to wait," she replied.

"Then I shall bid you goodbye," Doc said.

He was never one to pursue a futile effort.

"Mr. Weatherbee!"

"Yes, Miss Anderson."

"Well," she said, blushing, "I just wanted to say that I realize you acted on behalf of the Thomas family. Even in your... apparent indiscretions with Mrs. Wolcott."

"I'm so glad you realize that," Doc replied. "Now, if you'll excuse me..."

"Mr. Weatherbee."

"Yes."

"I'd be pleased to know how you dealt with the Thomases. I mean, to hear how you..."

"Of course," Doc replied. "But you'll have to excuse me for a moment."

"Where are you going?" she asked.

"To make sure my mule will be taken care of while I am away," he replied.

"Away?" she asked.

"Yes, I'm taking the next stage to Dodge City," he replied.

"Oh."

"I can't have you traveling alone," he replied. "It's not proper."

"Mr. Weatherbee, have you ever seen Washington?" she asked.

"No," Doc lied. "But I would like to."

"Would you mind if I walked with you to the livery?" she asked.

Doc extended his arm. Miss Anderson smiled and joined him. Together they strolled down the long wooden sidewalk.

JAKE LOGAN

___ 0-867-21087	**SLOCUM'S REVENGE**	$1.95
___ 07296-3	**THE JACKSON HOLE TROUBLE**	$2.50
___ 07182-0	**SLOCUM AND THE CATTLE QUEEN**	$2.75
___ 06413-1	**SLOCUM GETS EVEN**	$2.50
___ 06744-0	**SLOCUM AND THE LOST DUTCHMAN MINE**	$2.50
___ 07018-2	**BANDIT GOLD**	$2.50
___ 06846-3	**GUNS OF THE SOUTH PASS**	$2.50
___ 07046-8	**SLOCUM AND THE HATCHET MEN**	$2.50
___ 07258-4	**DALLAS MADAM**	$2.50
___ 07139-1	**SOUTH OF THE BORDER**	$2.50
___ 07460-9	**SLOCUM'S CRIME**	$2.50
___ 07567-2	**SLOCUM'S PRIDE**	$2.50
___ 07382-3	**SLOCUM AND THE GUN-RUNNERS**	$2.50
___ 07494-3	**SLOCUM'S WINNING HAND**	$2.50
___ 07493-5	**SLOCUM IN DEADWOOD**	$2.50

Prices may be slightly higher in Canada.

J.D. HARDEN

**"THE MOST EXCITING
WESTERN WRITER SINCE
LOUIS L'AMOUR"
—JAKE LOGAN**

____	872-16840-9	BLOOD, SWEAT AND GOLD	$1.95
____	872-16842-5	BLOODY SANDS	$1.95
____	867-21039-7	SONS AND SINNERS	$1.95
____	872-16869-7	THE SPIRIT AND THE FLESH	$1.95
____	867-21226-8	BOBBIES, BAUBLES AND BLOOD	$2.25
____	06572-3	DEATH LODE	$2.25
____	06138-8	HELLFIRE HIDEAWAY	$2.25
____	06380-1	THE FIREBRANDS	$2.25
____	06410-7	DOWNRIVER TO HELL	$2.25
____	06001-2	BIBLES, BULLETS AND BRIDES	$2.25
____	06331-3	BLOODY TIME IN BLACKTOWER	$2.25
____	06248-1	HANGMAN'S NOOSE	$2.25
____	06337-2	THE MAN WITH NO FACE	$2.25
____	06151-5	SASKATCHEWAN RISING	$2.25
____	06412-3	BOUNTY HUNTER	$2.50
____	06743-2	QUEENS OVER DEUCES	$2.50
____	07017-4	LEAD-LINED COFFINS	$2.50
____	06845-5	SATAN'S BARGAIN	$2.50
____	08013-7	THE WYOMING SPECIAL	$2.50
____	07259-2	THE PECOS DOLLARS	$2.50
____	07257-6	SAN JUAN SHOOTOUT	$2.50
____	07379-3	OUTLAW TRAIL	$2.50
____	07392-0	THE OZARK OUTLAWS	$2.50
____	07461-7	TOMBSTONE IN DEADWOOD	$2.50
____	07381-5	HOMESTEADER'S REVENGE	$2.50
____	07386-6	COLORADO SILVER QUEEN	$2.50

Prices may be slightly higher in Canada.

BERKLEY   *Available at your local bookstore or return this form to:*
Book Mailing Service
P.O. Box 690, Rockville Centre, NY 11571

Please send me the titles checked above. I enclose _____. Include 75¢ for postage and handling if one book is ordered; 25¢ per book for two or more not to exceed $1.75. California, Illinois, New York and Tennessee residents please add sales tax.

NAME_____

ADDRESS_____

CITY_____STATE/ZIP_____

(allow six weeks for delivery.)   **161**